AWARENESS

Book Two of the Influence Series

By David R. Bernstein

Bernstein, David R.
Awareness

ISBN-13: 978- 1983349324

For more information on reproducing sections of this book or sales of this book, go to www.davidrbernstein.com

10 9 8 7 6 5 4 3 2 1

Contents:

1
UNKNOWNS

FARREN REFUSES TO turn away, even as the wind from the FlexViper's blades whips up dirt into his eyes. I can't peel myself from the window as we lift further into the air. It was only a few days ago that we met, but losing him now feels cruel.

I need Amanda to be all right. She doesn't even know I'm leaving. The thought of losing her again distracts me enough to look away from Farren. Amanda is nowhere in sight, we're too high up now. The waning treetops conceal the Talas gates where I saw her last.

"You'll see them again," Jax says. "We'll come back, I promise."

A simple nod is all I can offer him.

The cabin of this craft is small, but quiet. Sleek lines and dull leather cover most of the panels that don't have digital displays or controls. Jax and I sit in the cramped rear row while Miya helms the pilot seat. Stratton swipes through a tablet in the front passenger seat.

Miya checks the controls, but the Viper is set to autopilot. These luxury play toys of the elite do not require you to know how to fly.

"Are our parents being treated well?" Jax looks to Miya.

Her eyes flicker back to him, but she never turns. "They're safe. The Vernon Society are not animals like the Magnus Order is...was."

"You guys wiped out a caravan of people just trying to get to me," I hiss. "How are you not animals? Do I have to remind you what that guy did?"

Stratton hardly budges at the comment, still fiddling with his device.

"I'm truly sorry for what you guys went through," Miya says softly. "What we are trying to do is far too important. It was the only way."

"Were you ever on our side?" Jax asks. An unfamiliar look of anger fills his face.

She adjusts a few controls, "Someone had to be there to nudge the resistance along. I secured my position with the Order so I could evaluate their personnel. It was the best way to find officers willing to defect."

"So you played on my weaknesses," Jax says. "You knew who I was all along. You knew I wanted to find my parents. You played with my emotions. I never really started the resistance—it was you all along, wasn't it?"

"I'm sorry, Jax," Miya says. "I'm sorry."

Jax leans back in his seat, turning to look out his window. I take his hand, but he doesn't turn to me.

The craft continues to ascend, the brightness of the sun reflecting off the white clouds as we soar above them. The intensity of the light activates the UV shielding on the windows. The cabin dims a bit, making it more comfortable.

"So what's the plan?" I ask Miya. "Do you think you will take us to our parents and then we will just take up your cause or whatever you guys call it?"

"Ugh, enough questions already," Stratton sighs. You'll do what we say you do... it's that simple."

I shift to him. His dark brow tightens. Lights from the displays reflect from his slicked-back, pitch-black hair. A few loose strands dangle across his forehead.

"How can you do what you do?" I ask. "Do you not have a soul?"

He drops the tablet into his lap and shifts in his seat to look at me. "Do you not understand what 'no more questions' means?"

"What do you feel when you darken someone's mind like that?" I ignore his request. "I felt what you do and if I can feel it, then it must consume every bit of you."

"Enough!" he snarls. "You know nothing about me. Go meddle in your brother's emotions. His sad puppy dog eyes are calling you."

I look to Jax; he's disconnected. I've not seen him like this before. His head is propped up against the side panel. In the last hour, he's learned his parents are alive and he has a sister. That plus he's been played for the last six months. This new bond we have has awakened something deeper. If he hurts, I hurt.

"We're going to figure this out together," I say. "Your... I mean our parents will have answers."

"Ya see, that's a much better use of your time," Stratton grins.

"Why don't you shut up, Stratton," Jax bites.

"Oh, *zen-boy* is getting feisty. Don't forget who's reuniting you with your mommy and daddy."

I release Jax's hand and sit up as far as the safety restraint will allow, "What's in this for you, Stratton? You don't seem like the loyal, castle wizard type."

"That's cute," he replies. "Does that make you the helpless princess in the tower?"

"Why are you doing this? Who made you like this?" I rest back in my seat, disgusted.

Stratton pauses for a second, unable to jab back. Something hit home with my last comment.

"Mind your own business," he says, turning back around.

No one's in the mood to talk anymore. Jax is overwhelmed. A child-like innocence replaces the strength his eyes normally convey. Miya's focused on navigation and controls or something. Stratton is stewing in his seat, like someone stole his lunch. I can do nothing but look back out the window. The beauty of the lush mountain ranges peek through the clouds we fly over. The clouds act like a barrier, holding down all the filth and pain from the surface. Exhaustion takes over and my eyes roll back.

***

"...because it matters," Miya says to Stratton, jolting me awake.

Rubbing my eyes, I try to clear the fog from my head. Jax is sleeping. He looks peaceful resting against the soft leather panel.

"Morning, sunshine," Stratton teases.

"Where are we?" I look out to find the scenery hasn't changed much.

Jax stirs, stiffening in his seat. Reality catches up with him as he calms down.

"This looks like Oregon," Jax says with a yawn as he peers out the window.

"Yeah, we're about twenty minutes out," Miya says.

"From where?" I ask.

"Seattle."

I've never been this far north before. Bordering sector groups control every road. Lost Souls is familiar. I know every inch of it—walked every road. But this, this is something new. New has not treated me well so far.

"Have you been?" I ask Jax.

"Yeah, Magnus had me and a few other Influencers scout as far north as Portland. They hoped we could secure more territory, but Harvesters and the Vernon Society are all over this area."

"Did you try looking for them—our parents?" I ask, knowing the answer.

"Ever Society outpost, every member we came across. Nothing."

"Alright, listen up," Stratton commands, his sight locked on that tablet. "When we arrive, you're both going to be processed by security as soon as you step off the Viper. I suggest you don't make this difficult."

Not sure why he would say that. We volunteered to come with them. Sure, they had guns pointing and threatened us with hurting our parents, but we're here now. No point in fighting, anymore.

"If our parents are safe, you have nothing to worry about," Jax says.

"Oh, you'll know soon enough," Stratton smirks.

"What does that mean?" I ask.

"It just means you will get to see them shortly after we get there." Miya shakes her head at Stratton.

"Prepare for final decent. We will arrive at your destination in approximately ten minutes," a pleasant female voice relays from the FlexViper's front panel.

The blinding whiteness makes way for an unfamiliar sight—rain clouds. Condensation collects on the windows. Tiny droplets vertically stream across the side of our craft before the velocity of the Viper whisks them away. Variants of grey ripple across the horizon, making it hard to see much of anything. No sky or mountains—just dullness. Lost Souls rarely gets rain anymore. The last time was over five years ago. It wasn't much to speak of. Even with the uncertainties we face, I take a moment to soak in something new.

"Heads up." Miya points out the right side of the FlexViper.

I pull myself over as far as I can, nearly spreading across Jax's lap. Out his window, a daunting skyline peaks through the cloud cover. Countless skyscrapers emerge. There's no power feeding what I assume is Seattle. All the windows on the structures are dark giving the feel of geometric mountains cutting at every angle. Lifeless and ominous, but every city I've been to is far from lifeless. Amanda and I have avoided every large city. If the Harvesters don't find you, some deviant sector group will.

"There it is," Stratton says, squinting out the front.

A simple but towering building stands out from the rest. A large red cross, which must be a landing pad, covers the rooftop.

"Welcome to the Vernon Society," Miya says.

2

THE SOCIETY

MEN WITH RIFLES stand firm at each corner. Dark, long coats and beanies appear to be the Society's choice for outfits. We hover several yards above the pad as the Viper, on its own, edges closer, steadying itself. My core flutters as nervous energy fills my body. Jax firmly grips my hand almost as if he's trying to pull the fear from me.

"I'm here," Jax whispers. "We'll do this together."

I purse my lips and offer him a nod. That familiar ease has returned to his eyes, portraying the comfort that I desperately need at this moment.

Not more than a subtle rattle and we've landed. The Viper hisses and beeps as it shuts down.

Unbuckling, Stratton turns to us, "Don't move. The security team will escort you in when they're ready."

Miya pops her door, and frigid air pours in, forcing me to shudder. I pull away from Jax and tightly draw my arms in. It offers little to fend off the freezing air. I'm not used to this.

Miya is greeted by a pale-faced man, his rifle stowed at his side. Offering her a hand, he guides her from the Viper and onto the rooftop. He returns a few moments later with a thin blanket that he hands me. I yank it from him, franticly wrapping it around my shoulders. The same man with his expressionless face offers me his hand.

"Go… I'm right behind you," Jax says.

Refusing to take the guard's hand, I crawl out the small opening on my own. The man gestures me toward a door off in the corner of the roof that Miya stands before. She's now wearing one of those stiff coats like the rest of them. I stand just outside the craft and wait for Jax. A different guard, shorter and stockier then the one next to me, instructs him to exit. He steps out and without hesitating, he comes to my side, wrapping his arm around my shivering shoulders.

"Let's do this," he says, staring straight at Miya.

Stratton is the last out of the Viper. He refuses to look at us. As if he's done his job and can finally go. The guards get out of his way as he storms past them toward the door. Miya steps aside and he vanishes through the entry.

Miya waves for us to come over. However, it's the guards, hulking behind us with weapons in hand, that encourage us to move.

The open door leads to a stairwell. Miya leads the way down. The clanking footsteps on the metal staircase echo off the dull cement walls that surround us.

"So, where are we headed to?" I ask, watching as motion-sensor lights flicker the lower we go. This building seems to have functioning power. Or, at least, working generators.

"We're taking you to your quarters," Miya says. "You must be tired. I know I am."

She speaks to me as if we're still on the same side. Like we are still friends—or whatever we were.

"I want to see my parents now," Jax insists.

"There will be plenty of time for that," Miya says. "You guys need to rest and maybe eat something. They're not ready for you."

"Not ready for us?" I ask, carefully watching my footsteps as we continue down the stairs. "What does that mean?"

"I'm just saying you will have your reunion in time."

Miya stops at a door marked 'Level 32'. She steps aside to let one of the guards slide a key card into a black panel near the door's handle. With a pop followed by a soft beep, it opens. I tilt my head to sneak a look at what's inside. A dim-lit hall, with regal-looking wooden doors, lines each side.

"What is this place?" Jax asks.

"McCaw Tower," the taller guard says, gesturing us to enter. "Luxury livin' at its finest."

A camera is mounted in the corner above us. It pans over in our direction as the door opens. I guess it makes sense for the Vernon Society's headquarters to be in a condo complex. Advanced security, rooftop access, fancy living quarters, and I'm sure a few Influencers containing the Harvester population outside. It's a perfect place to do evil.

We walk for several yards before the guard stops us, pulling out a different keycard.

"This is your suite," he says to me in a raspy voice.

"Wait, I'm not leaving Jax," I say.

"It's ok," Miya says to the taller guard. "Let them stay together. There's plenty of room."

"Thank you," Jax says to her, polite as always.

The guard opens the door, stuffing the keycard back into his pocket. I guess we don't get access to the snack machine we passed down the hall.

"So, we're prisoners?" I ask.

"You're guests," Miya says. "We're just keeping you guys safe."

"Yeah, whatever."

With no other options, Jax and I walk into the suite. A short entry hall gives way to an expansive room with a huge four-pane window stretching across most of the back wall. Leather couches face a gigantic TV mounted between two doors that must lead to bedrooms. A full kitchen with shiny appliances and marble countertops is nestled into the right corner. I've only seen this type of luxury in old magazines that litter the streets.

"The staff will bring you dinner shortly," Miya says from outside the suite. "The building has full power and heated water. Take a shower. Relax, watch some movies."

"What's the point of this?" Jax asks. "When can we see our parents?"

"Jax," Miya sighs. "My friendship with you was never fake. I'm just working toward something bigger and better. Tomorrow it will all make sense, when you speak with your parents."

"Now it's tomorrow?" he snarls. "This is not ok."

Jax motions as if he's going toward the exit when the two guards step in to block him.

"You might be our guests, but you haven't earned our trust, yet," the stocky guard says, expressionless.

"Jax…" I pull on his wrist. "…it's fine. Let's catch our breath for a minute, okay?"

I know there's no way we're going to be allowed to just roam this building freely. We need time to figure out things—time to recoup.

"Fine," he narrows his eyes on the man. "We would like to be left alone now."

"Boys," Miya insists. "Let's give them some space. Let them decompress a bit."

The men relax their stance. The taller of the two grabs the heavy-looking door as the other returns to Miya. Without another word, he shuts it, an electronic clank followed by a beep escapes from the handle.

A deep exhale slips from my chest without warning. I flop down on the smooth, cold couch. Exhausted and overwhelmed, I look to Jax, hoping for some of that insightful, calming wisdom. I get nothing but an empty stare out the window.

"Hey," I plead. "You still with me?"

Reawakened by my words, he looks at me as he drags himself to the couch. He groans as he allows his body to fall to the far end. Clearly the weight of the day is affecting him.

"I'm sorry," he whispers, his hand covers his eyes. "Let's just rest a minute and then we'll figure this out."

***

A muffled knock startles me awake. Someone's at the entrance. Shaking the fog from my head, I turn to find Jax already up and heading to the door. I'm not sure if he slept or not. Placing his face close, he peaks through the peephole before pulling back.

"It's someone with food," he says.

I sit up. "Let them in. We haven't eaten since this morning. There's no point in a hunger strike. We're useless with no energy."

"Please return to the couch," a deep voice calls from behind the door.

"Return to the couch?" I whisper to Jax. "How did they…"

Jax stops me and points to another camera mounted in the corner above the door. My brain is fried. I've already forgotten we saw it when we entered. I'm not used to being watched.

Jax returns to the couch, sitting right next to me this time. He's protecting me.

The same clank and beep come from the door as a new guard enters. A man struts in, wearing that familiar coat, minus the beanie this time. His perfectly-parted brown hair and clean-shaven face give him a look of importance. He shifts his blue eyes onto me. A young boy enters behind him, pushing a cart filled with platters covered with silver lids and several drinks in fine looking glassware. This kid looks no older than twelve or thirteen. He refuses to look at us almost as if he's ashamed of what he's doing. Or maybe he's been told not to. Neither of these people enter my awareness. Just like the guards on the rooftop, they all have the block implants.

"Our kitchen has prepared quite a feast for you two," the guard says in a calm, but assertive tone. "Eat up and someone will return in the morning to take you to your parents."

He turns, signaling the boy to leave. The guard doesn't say another word as he follows the kid out of the suite.

I rush to the cart and pull it to the couch. The food's not going to be poisoned. That would be pointless to bring us here just to kill us in style.

Under the first silver cover, a spread of meats and cheeses fill every inch of the large white plate. I pull off the next cover to find a bounty of perfectly ripe fruits and crisp vegetables. The array of color is unlike anything I've seen before. Finally, under the last cover, a decadent sampling of chocolate treats fan-out in a spiraling presentation, so mouthwatering and beautiful that I can hardly contain my excitement.

I'm the first to dig in, grabbing a handful of the cake before stuffing it into my mouth. A rich, nutty flavor explodes, sending my taste buds into overdrive. Jax looks at me with a puzzled grin.

"What?" I mumble.

We don't speak for several minutes as we clean nearly every speck of food off this cart.

Resting our heads back on the couch now, we try to settle our full bellies.

"Did you feel anything outside?" Jax asks, wiping chocolate from his mouth.

"What do you mean? Besides the Harvester wall that their Influencers have formed around this building?"

We didn't even need to talk about this. I am sure, just like me, he scanned the area with his Push ability right when we got here and noticed the awareness of hundreds of implant-free Harvesters pacing around outside. Their mood is calm and emotionless. The Society has obviously tamed them for security.

"No, not that," he says. "Have you tried to push them yet?"

"No. I just felt around, why?"

"I've tried several times to alter their states," he says, sitting up now. "But each time I do, my Push is defused or something."

"What do you mean?" I ask. "Do you think they have strong Influencers blocking you?"

He stands and walks to the windows, staring out at the blacked out city below.

"It's different," he says. "It's easy to break them from the Society's manipulation, but when I try to shape them, my Push stops working, like I've lost my ability."

Great, not only do they have Stratton and his evil powers, but the Vernon Society seems to have someone who can neuter others' Push abilities.

3

REUNION

I HAVEN'T SLEPT in a bed that wasn't just a thin cot or pile of blankets on the ground for as long as I can remember. Amanda and I could both sleep on this and never even touch. It's huge.

It took a while to fall asleep last night. All I could think of was Amanda and Ava. Both are alone now. Sure they have Farren and the rest of the resistance, but Ava lost her love, Maddux. I can't imagine how she must be feeling. Amanda's strong, but her life for the last six years was protecting me. We need each other. Farren will take care of her, but that doesn't fill the void left in my chest. My breath shortens as I fight back the emotions.

I avoid thinking too much about Farren. It's too overwhelming. I need to stay focused for Jax. He's family and needs me more than anyone right now.

I crawl out of the soft, warm bed and make my way to the bathroom. Looking in the mirror, I cringe at my appearance. The shower last night before bed was amazing—warm and soothing. I was able to clean off weeks of grime and filth, but my hair is still a mess. Brushing it out is painful with all the tangles and knots. The luxurious bathroom has everything a girl would need to pamper herself. Not that I've ever pampered myself before, or even know where to start.

Digging around in one of the many drawers, I find a pair of scissors. Normally Amanda would be here to do this, but my hair is too unmanageable now. I have to take care of it. I gather my hair into a ponytail and pull it over my shoulder. With one clean cut from the sharp sheers, five or six inches of rat's nest fall to the marble floor. Instantly the weight is lifted. Looking at my reflection, my hair lays just past my shoulders now. It's uneven, though. Trying my best, I'm able to clean it up, snipping a bit here and some more there. Not perfect, but better.

I throw the scissors back in the drawer and grab the brush. It flows through with little effort. It feels so much nicer. What to do with it now? I could just throw it back up into a ponytail, but I'm kind of tired of that. It's been that way for years. Farren pops in my head. What would he like? I need to stop—that's silly now. Rummaging through a cabinet next to the mirror, I find a tube of something called calming crème. The bottle reads that it calms frizzy hair. Well, I definitely have that going on. I squeeze some in my hand and pull it through my hair. I have no idea what I'm doing. Its scent reminds me of the fresh fruit we ate last night. Grabbing the brush, I give my hair another once over. The cream dries fairly quick. I tousle my hair with my fingers a few times. That's it, I'm done. It doesn't look half bad. I leave my newly tamed hair down. No more ponytails.

"Hey," Jax calls from outside my room. "They brought us breakfast."

People bringing me food is just odd. I used to be lucky if I got to eat at all.

I straighten my top and head to the door. "Coming."

Opening my bedroom door, I find a new cart filled with more of those silver, covered trays. My attention is drawn to the couch. There's a pillow and blanket neatly folded at the end.

"Did you sleep on the couch?" I ask.

"Yeah, I didn't want any surprises," he says, peaking inside the trays. "I don't care how much they pretend we are guests. We need to be careful."

"You should've told me. I would've stayed out here with you."

"Nah, you needed your sleep. You've been through enough."

I smile. He's so thoughtful, but I bet reuniting with his parents, our parents, had him up most of the night thinking.

Today's bounty is waffles, more fresh fruit, and what smells like real scrambled eggs. Fluffy and a subtle yellow color help me realize they are for sure real. Been a long time.

I ate so much last night that I actually don't have an appetite. My stomach is not used to eating like that. It's a shame, everything smells so good. Might as well pick at it.

"Did the guard say anything about taking us to our parents?" I ask, nibbling on a bright red strawberry.

"Yeah," he digs into the eggs. "They're going to take us up at 9am."

"I know this is hard," I say. "You going to be ok with all of this?"

"I'll be okay, promise. Oh, hey, they dropped off some clothes for you," he points to a bag near the door. "I guess they figured a tank top is not the proper outfit for the Pacific Northwest."

I take a sip of some vibrant orange juice. Pulpy and delicious, it's hard not to guzzle it all, even if I'm not hungry. The white bag looks like it came from one of those department store's that people would shop at before the world fell apart. I've seen these bags all over Lost Souls. Only, they are not used for such nice, new things. I grab the bag, looking inside. Digging through, I pull out a pair of dark jeans, a blue top, and black jacket. They all look to be my size. I'm a little creeped out they know this.

"Do you mind?" I raise the bag to Jax.

"No problem, we've got about fifteen minutes before they come for us."

I head into the bathroom and quickly undress. The jeans slip on perfectly. It feels nice and new. I sniff the top, checking its freshness. It's a little stronger, but the floral scent reminds me of laundry day at the orphanage. I loved that day. You just feel more human with clean clothes. I'm not fighting this. The old rags I've been wearing for the last couple of days were getting ripe. Can't go getting all showered up and clean only to wear the same stinky clothes. A new outfit is not going to turn me into a Vernon Society minion. I toss the old outfit into the trash can next to the sink and go back to the living room.

Jax looks up and smiles. "Looks nice."

"Thanks."

I didn't notice when I first saw him this morning, but he has a new outfit too. Dark fitted jeans, a white t-shirt, and a light blue jacket that brings out the brightness in his eyes. Those eyes do look familiar the more I notice them. The lightness of the irises is definitely a family trait.

"Listen," Jax steps close to me. "Just play along and when the time is right we will find a way out of this. All of us."

I nod, shifting my eyes to the camera. We have to remember they are watching and most likely listening to everything we do in this room.

Almost as if on cue, the lock on the door clicks. We both take a step back. No warning this time as they walk in. The same proper looking guard who brought us dinner escorts Miya, sporting a fresh bandage on her head wound. The guard's coat flaps open revealing a pistol strapped to his waist. Right behind them, a beautiful girl walks in, crimson red hair bouncing with every step. She's not wearing the Society apparel the rest of them wear. Her outfit is similar to mine: jeans, a fitted top and a dark leather jacket. She avoids eye contact with us.

"Good morning," Miya smiles. "Hope you slept well."

"We slept fine," Jax replies, brows tightened.

"I don't think you've been properly introduced to this gentleman." She reaches up to rest a hand on his shoulder. "This is Captain Relic; he is head of security for the Society. And this young lady back here is my assistant, Neira."

She still refuses to look at us or even make an expression, as she stands there, arms folded.

"Can we go now?" Jax pleads.

"Of course, of course," Miya says, placing her hands into her coat pockets. "Please, follow me."

We head out of the suite and into the hall. Relic falls back to trail behind us. He seems more concerned about us than Miya. Neira keeps pace with Jax and I, almost mirroring our steps.

We reach the end of the hall but instead of entering the stairwell we stand in front of an elevator door.

"Sorry we couldn't use this last night when we arrived," Miya says, pushing the up button. "There are restrictions on its use."

"You are taking us to our parents, right?" Jax asks. "I'm done waiting."

Relic huffs. "Relax, we're taking you to them now. Remember who's in charge here."

"It's ok, Captain," Miya grins softly. "This is a big day for them. Their lives are about to change."

She seems too confident that we will just see our parents and all will magically be fine. As if we won't fight with every bit of our ability to free them.

The elevator door beeps and slides open. Mirrored panels line every wall inside. Miya extends her hand out, gesturing for us to enter. Jax is first to walk in. I follow right behind him. The rest of them file in, standing in front of us, facing the door as it slides closed. Miya pushes the highest floor button—the fifty-eighth floor.

Why would we be going to the top floor to see our parents? They better not be ambushing us with recruitment crap from the leadership.

A soft ding sounds as we pass each floor. No one is talking or moving much. I swallow as fear has reentered my body. A soft exhale helps a bit, but this slow ride up is freaking me out. Jax mouths to me that we will be okay. Having him here makes this far less terrifying.

One final ding and we've reached the fifty-eighth floor. The doors whoosh open. I stretch my neck to see around Captain Relic's broad shoulders. An elegant hall emerges, lined with small, narrow tables on each side, decorated with fresh flowers. Marble dons the ceiling and walls. Arched and at least ten feet tall, this entryway is impressive.

We step out, one by one. There's only one door and it stands at the end of this short walkway. Carved wood paneling and shiny gold plating emit a sense of power and importance.

Jax takes my hand, leading me forward. This has to be nerve-racking for him. He's been waiting four years for this moment.

"Alright guys," Miya says, stopping before the door. "This is where I leave you for now. I truly hope you find what you're looking for."

She walks back to the elevator and presses the button. The door opens immediately. She enters alone, leaving Captain Relic and Neira behind.

Relic pulls a tethered keycard from his pocket. The metal chain scrapes against his holstered pistol as he waves it pass the entry panel. A green light blips on and off before a soft click comes from the door.

"Remember, we're watching you." Relic opens the thick door, strutting in and out of sight.

An expansive room opens up in front of us. We step forward onto an intricate mosaic tiled entryway. Spiraled lines fan out as they intertwine with delicate patterns.

Huge square tiles line every inch of this room's flooring. Everything's shiny and expensive looking. Pillars connect the tiled floor to the wood-paneled, vaulted ceilings. The lighting in this room makes everything shimmer.

"This way," Relic insists.

He stands in front of a door off of this main room. Neira still shadows us, waiting for our next move. We follow him to the entry.

Relic leads us down a narrow hall that's decorated with unique paintings, each one more expensive looking then the next. Not that there's money anymore. Power is the new currency of the country. The Vernon Society looks to be bathing in power.

"They're waiting for you in the study," Relic says, pointing to the closed door before us.

He steps aside, letting us go to the door on our own. Neira stops trailing us too. She stands at the far end of the corridor, leaning against the wall. I don't think they are going too far from this room.

I turn to Jax. "You ready to do this?"

"I hope so," he replies.

Grabbing the stiff handle, I pause for a moment before wrenching it down. It swings open with little effort. Sitting on a chair in front of a sprawling shelf full of books, an older man with salt and pepper hair straightens. Thin, but not overly thin. A well-groomed white beard fills out his face. Catching my eye, his mouth drops just a bit before a soft smile warms up his expression.

"Jax?" A soft voice asks from the opposite side of the room. "Is that you?"

A woman with dark-blond hair, highlighted by grey streaks, stands near the large wooden desk at the back of this office, her face filled with wonder.

"Mom?" Jax's voice stammers. "Is it really you?"

"It is... it is," she says, slowly walking toward us.

Jax moves closer, hesitant but eager at the same time. They meet in the middle of the room. Towering over her, Jax peers down for a second before wrapping his arms around her. She melts into his chest.

"Kaylin?" The man asks, standing now. "I'm so glad you're here. Wow, you look just like her."

I turn to the lady holding Jax. I don't really see it.

"Are you my father?" The word 'father' gives me chills the moment it spills from my lips.

"That's what they tell me." He walks toward me. "Can I look at you, Dear?"

My mind races with competing emotions. Fear, confusion, excitement, unease—the full array. I nod as I glance at him. I realize Jax and I never spoke about them last night. We were too distracted, I guess.

"My word." He sighs as he looks me over. "You're beautiful."

"Um, thanks." I retreat a bit.

"You must have so many questions," he says.

He reaches down to take my wrist, but I pull away without even noticing. His lips purse, a subtle grin forms.

"Oh, forgive me," he says.

"I'm sorry," I say. "I didn't mean to."

"It's fine, Kaylin. I understand completely."

"Kaylin," the older lady says. "I've waited so long to see you."

Walking over, she clasps Jax's hand, pulling him with her. I don't think she wants to let go again.

"Hi," is all I can offer.

"My name is Laney, I'm your mother."

"I'm sorry, I really don't know what to say here." Nerves turn to uncertainty.

"It's okay, dear," she says. "Can we sit?"

I nod and she leads us to a regal looking couch in front of an idle fireplace. She sits in the middle, forcing Jax and I to take the spots next to her. The man stands behind the couch and rests a hand on Jax's shoulder. Jax reaches up to hold it.

Look at us, one big *happy* family. A family of strangers—abandoned children and absentee parents. Buried feelings start to bubble to the surface. Something I've never had to deal with before.

"I'm sorry," I snap. "Is someone going to talk about it? About why I was abandoned?"

I sit forward, wanting to run. Wanting to take Jax's hand and drag him out of this office and away from this odd setup for what feels like a family photoshoot. At any minute, I'm waiting for Neira to bust out a camera.

"We had no choice." Laney places a hand on my knee. "Your father and I lost of piece of ourselves that day. Recruiters from Magnus were coming for you. We wanted you to have a chance at freedom. A blank slate."

I push her hand away. "Why would a sector group come for a three-year-old? That makes no sense."

"You don't know who you are..." The man who says he's my father pauses. "...who your family is."

"What does that mean?" I hiss.

"Our family is tied to the start of all of this," Laney says. "The way the world is now, that's my sister's fault. Your Aunt Leeyah... she destroyed this country. She's the reason we live like savage monsters at war."

"I don't remember an Aunt Leeyah, Mom." Jax leans back from her. "How can one person be the cause of all of this?"

"She was a powerful Influencer, just like you two, but she was ruthless. I didn't want you to carry this burden. I didn't..."

My father interrupts Laney who is becoming emotional. "When she was young, she joined a terrorist group that set the country on fire. At the end, her Push ability was used to dissolve the foundation of society. She went crazy and took it out on us all."

"So, what, I'm guilty by association? Because of this, you just dump me on the steps of a shelter and wipe your hands of it?"

I stand and head toward the door when Laney rises to her feet, heading straight for me.

"Please," Laney begs, reaching for me. "You don't understand. Magnus knew about our family. They've been watching us for years. They hoped we would have children. Wanted my genes—wanted a weapon for their greedy ambitions."

"I have faint memories of a little girl that I would play with... was that Kaylin?" Jax turns to face his father. "I never knew who she was or why you guys brought her around. She just stopped coming to play with me one day. Why keep her so long, if you were just going to abandon her? Why did you decide to keep me?"

"Son, we made a deal with Magnus that our first born would be left alone. A deal that meant we needed to provide them with another child. I'm... I'm so sorry, but we couldn't follow through with it. We had to do something."

"Talik, please," Laney calls out to my father. "Let me handle this. It was my decision, my burden."

Relic enters, stretching his head in from beyond the open door. "Is everything alright?"

"Yes, yes, leave us now," Laney hisses.

Relic nods and without another word leaves the room, closing the door behind him. Almost as if he had no other choice but to listen to her.

"So, you just decided to have me and then you, what, changed your minds?" My voice shakes, heart racing.

"We did something horrible." Laney drops her head, pulling her hands to her temples. "We... we stole an orphan from the shelter the day you were born. We had no choice. We didn't want them taking Jax. We couldn't give you to them either."

A silence fills the room. Jax's eyes are wide, he backs up to the wall near the fireplace.

Talik has guilt written all over his face, but Laney is calm, almost unfazed. She looks like she's more disappointed about having to reveal her secret than disgusted by what she's done. Anger changes her mothering look; her eyes narrow and a faint, but noticeable frown forms.

"So, you steal a kid and still get rid of me," I say. "How does that work?"

Laney turns back and sits on the armrest of the couch, just a few feet from me. The calmness in her face returns. "They figured it out, I don't know how, but they got a genetic sample from our family. They knew the child we stole and gave them was not mine. They were coming for Jax."

"You were three at the time," Talik says to me. "We had to do something. Had to keep you out of their hands."

He turns to Jax, "We had to raise her in secret. We had a close friend pretend you were hers. We couldn't let them know about her or they would've figured out our deception. We called her by a different name and let you play with her from time to time. It was the best we could do."

Jax walks up to my side, careful not to overwhelm me. He gently rests his hand on my shoulder. I lean into his body and release the fourteen years of emotion hidden inside of me.

4

BIGGER PICTURE

JAX AND I sit on the hearth of the fireplace, side by side. Hands interlocked. I've been crying for a few minutes. Talik and Laney sit on the couch waiting. I don't think they want to throw anything else at us right now.

"Why did you have to make a deal with them, Dad?" Jax nods toward the door where Captain Relic stands guard. "Why did they take you?"

Talik looks at Laney, she nods as if she's giving him permission to respond.

"We disappeared after, you know, leaving Kaylin. It worked too, until your ability emerged. We had no choice. If we didn't go with them they would take you. Your mother is not able to have children anymore. So, instead of forcing us to give them a child they forced us to come work with them instead."

"At first, they ran genetic tests on me," Laney says, resting a hand on Talik's hand. "They hoped they could find the Influencer gene, but the science is just not there yet. Genetically creating Influencers is impossible. We don't test for that anymore."

"*We* don't test for that anymore?" I ask. "Who's we?"

Laney pauses for a moment, looking at Talik as if searching for the right words. "I took over as chairman of the Society ten months ago."

Jax springs to his feet, releasing my hand. The confusion pulls his body in all directions as he paces the room.

Laney's words send shockwaves down my spine, tightening my core, freezing me in place.

"Wait-wait-wait." Jax paces in front of me. "You're telling me you're the leader of this group? I don't understand. What's going on here?"

"Yes, Dear," Laney says to Jax. "We knew the only way to see you again was to take control of this group."

"I've been at war with the Vernon Society ever since I joined them years ago. Are you telling me I've been fighting my parents the whole time?"

I stand and reach for him, but he's unable to stay in one place. He doesn't even notice.

"Son," Talik says. "We found out you were part of the Magnus order only months after we took over."

"How did you even take over?" I interrupt.

"Yeah, how do you go from being forced to join them, to running the group?" Jax asks.

Laney stands and steps toward Jax. He backs up. She stops and returns to the couch. She didn't even come to me, didn't even look to see if I was ok.

Laney sits again and looks at me. "The Society is different from most sector groups. It's a democracy of sorts. We earned their trust by doing everything we were asked. Before long, we were one of them—adding value to the group. The former chairman passed away and a vote was held. I put my name in the race and won."

"So, once you found out I was working with Magnus, you put this whole manufactured resistance plan into place? Why? Was I more valuable as an unwilling pawn then a son?"

"Of course not," Talik insists. "We knew they would never just let you leave. The only way was to topple them. And that started from the inside out."

Jax turns quiet. His eyes run back and forth like he is processing the moment. What they say makes sense, but there are still so many unanswered questions.

"What about me," I say. "Was I just an inconvenient bump in the road? Was I ever a part of the plans?"

"It's not like that." Laney shifts to me. "We knew you were somewhere in Lost Souls, but you kept off the radar for so long. It must have been fate that you two found each other."

Something doesn't feel right about this. It's all too convenient. You don't put your children at risk in a deadly resistance if you want them back alive.

"Are you guys the reason every sector group has been looking for me?" I ask, swallowing down the lump that's formed in my throat. "I mean, I did one Push when I was eleven. No one should be looking for me six years later."

Laney's head tilts ever so slightly at my question. Her eyes narrow on me. I'm not sure if the reaction is disappointment or confusion.

"We didn't mean to make a region-wide manhunt for you. But we did spread the word about you, hoping you might pop up so we could bring you home safely."

"That's just dumb." The words pour out on their own. "I've been living in fear every day for the last six years. Not knowing if one day someone would find me and force me to control people against their will. My life's been hell. And now you tell me you made the manhunt even worse. What if the Southern Alliance found me? They treat their Influencers like crap—like slaves. How dare you."

"Do not talk to me like that, young lady." Laney's voice bites with fire. "You've been on the run because of those abilities, not because we've been looking for you. We brought you home for something bigger. We're going to give your life purpose. You need to know your place here. Understand who you are talking to."

"MOM!" Jax shouts. "Why are you treating her like this? She has every right to figure out the missing pieces of her life."

From time to time I would picture what it would be like to meet my Mom and Dad. Have them tear up at the sight of me. It would be like life never skipped a beat and we would be family again. This does not feel like that— at all.

"You're right, she does," Laney says to Jax. "But this war has forced us to take drastic measures to bring you home. Bring you both home I mean."

"Why did you have them tell us that the Society was holding you against your will?" I ask, looking back and forth between Laney and Talik.

Once again, Talik looks to Laney seeking approval to answer. She again nods, allowing him to speak.

"We've propped up your resistance for months," Talik answers. "We couldn't throw that away. The Magnus Order was eating away at our reach. Digging into our territory. If we didn't take them down, they would control half of the country." He turns his attention to Jax. "If Jax knew we were alive and thriving, he might not have been motivated to lead you guys to victory. We had to let it play out."

"Once we heard they found you..." Laney looks at me, eyes welling up with emotion. "...we knew we had our chance to bring our family back together. Now that you're both here we can achieve so much more."

Laney cautiously walks to Jax, extending her arms to him. Jax pauses for a moment, but accepts her embrace. She reaches a hand out to me, wanting me to join them, but I can't, it doesn't feel right. I feel like an accident. Like I've always been a burden for their family. Talik walks over to them. Towering over Laney, he wraps his thin arms around them both. I once again stand alone, out of place in the world.

Jax pulls away from them and walks to me. He avoids my eyes. Without hesitating, he pulls me into his body, wrapping me up in his soothing awareness. It feels nice, comfortable.

"Now, we need to talk about how we're going to save this country," Laney says with a determined look of ambition erasing the mothering look she just had.

"What?" I scoff. "I don't understand you. You just got your kids back. Don't you want to get to know me or see how life's been for Jax?"

Laney folds her arms. I must be in trouble. Maybe she'll *ground* me.

"Kaylin, life isn't a beautiful movie with a perfect ending. This world is sick and with the help of you two, we can begin the healing process. Rebuild a stable country."

"With our help?" I ask, confused. "How can two people save the country? Why does it feel like family is secondary with you?"

"Kaylin." Talik steps to the side of Laney. "Please understand everything is about family. We want a world where you both can live a normal, happy life. Not one where you're hiding and fighting until something worse happens."

Jax pulls away from me. It felt nice to have someone to count on, family to trust. My parents don't give me that same feeling, yet.

"Dad," Jax says to Talik. "What are you guys trying to do here? How are you going to save the country?"

"We have a plan, son," Talik says. "We will unify all Influencers and heal this fractured country."

Laney steps in front of Talik and says, "With all Influencers fighting for the Society we will end this endless sector war. Stop the constant greed that destroyed society."

"What does that mean?" I take another step back. "You want your own Influencer army?"

"Yes, Kaylin. Think about it. All your kind working together... under my guidance. We can achieve so much together."

They're insane. They just want to use us. A deep regret pulls the air from my lungs, pinning it in my stomach. Coming here was a mistake.

"Our *kind* Mom?" Jax's brow tightens.

"Yes, Dear, I mean people like you. And I want you to lead them. Join our family again and end this nightmare."

"Jax, this is crazy," I plead to him. "What makes this any better than Magnus or the Southern Alliance?

Everyone just uses us to control things. She just wants to use us like the rest of them."

Confusion consumes Jax's face. His eyes shift from side to side as he tries to digest everything. His calming essence is once again ripped from him, replaced by an agonizing confliction. I reach out to touch him, but he folds his arm and turns away from me.

"Kaylin, they're our parents," Jax says, avoiding the desperation in my eyes that begs for him to leave with me. "I've been fighting for so long. There has to be something better for us."

Laney walks to him. She pulls loose his tightly locked arms. They fall to his side as she wraps her arms around his mid-section, pulling herself in close. He hesitates for a second, but can't resist. He hugs her back, gently resting his head on top of hers.

"We can do this, son." Laney looks up at him.

Talik cautiously walks to me, a calmness fills his face. Wrinkles form around his eyes as he softly smiles. The course and grey beard somehow gives him an inviting look. He has a warmth to him that Laney doesn't have. He takes both my hands into his own.

"Just give us a chance to get to know you. I've thought of you every day since we had to give you up. I know you're unsure of things, but hang around a few days. You're not a prisoner here. You're family."

"So, you're not going to make me stay?" I ask, not trusting what I'm hearing.

"You guys are very important to us," Laney says. "We need you both."

That wasn't the most comforting way to keep me here, but nothing Laney has said feels mothering anyway. She has a fondness for Jax, but it doesn't appear to spill over to me.

"So, what now?" I ask, feeling confused and anxious.

Laney pulls away from Jax. She holds one of his hands and pulls him toward me. With her free hand she takes mine and stands between us.

"Now you rest and when you're ready, we will move forward. Until then, take advantage of the facility. What's ours is yours."

"I need time to think about all of this," Jax says, releasing Laney's hand. "I need to get out of here."

"I'll go with you," I say.

"No, I need to be alone. Please understand Kaylin."

"Take all the time you need," Laney says to him. "Level 32 is empty and just for you guys."

He nods and heads to the door before turning back to look at me. He says nothing before walking out. A heavy weight drags at my core. I'm alone again.

5

A VISIT

THE SUITE FEELS empty without Jax. The lunch trays remain untouched. I don't feel hungry. All I can think of is Jax and what's on his mind. My so-called parents aren't what I expected at all. The special moment was nothing more than a recruiting session for some crazy world domination plan.

Staring out the window, I fiddle with the necklace around my neck. The hope it once represented is gone, replaced by something hallow. It was nothing more than a tool for Laney to verify my identity. I yank it down, breaking the delicate links. Balling it up in my hands, I squeeze it tightly in frustration. I toss it to the ground in the corner. It no longer has any value to me.

Heavy thuds startle me from my overthinking. Someone's at the door. They didn't just enter on their own this time. That's something. The unknowns still seize my insides, making my heart race.

Walking slowly to the door, I gently rest my hands on the cool surface and peak through the peephole. Stratton and Neira stand side by side, staring right at me through the hole. I quickly step back to the side. My breathing picks up, leaving no gaps in between breaths.

"Come on, open it already," Stratton says, in his customary annoyed tone. "Mommy sent us to talk to you."

Thoughts jump from my mind. I have nothing to say to him. He's heartless and just plain evil. Just because they want me to join their *team*, doesn't make me forget what he did.

"Helloooo?" Stratton sings.

I can't hide in here forever. Jax would know what to do.

"Hold on," I say, leaning up against the only exit.

My hand slides down the door, clasping onto the mechanical latch. A deep exhale distracts me long enough to shut my brain off, allowing me to open the door. I pull slowly on the brass handle, hoping they will have disappeared by the time it is fully open. No such luck.

"Hi there, Princess." Stratton gives a sarcastic bow.

Neira rolls her eyes as Stratton chuckles.

"Nice place," Stratton boasts. "Oh and lunch is served. I'm starving."

Stratton pulls the food tray past me as he walks backward. I lean against the door as he forces his way by. The casters squeak as they roll on the delicate carpeting in the living area. He slams it into the arm of the leather couch, bringing it to a complete stop.

Neira walks in behind him and sits at the wood-lined lounge chair nearest to the window. Staring out, she looks caught up in her own world.

Stratton plops down in front of the tray, opening each shiny cover. He moans at each new tasty discovery he tries.

"Now this is livin'," he says, wiping chocolate cream from his mouth.

"What do you want?" I stand in the middle of the room, arms folded.

He shoves down a mouthful and washes it down with a swig of orange juice. "Mother Dearest thinks we Influencers need to bond or something. I on the other hand, don't need *Luke* and *Leia* to get in my way."

"Who's Luke and Leia?" I ask.

"Really? Oh, never mind."

"Jace, enough already," Neira says calmly, turning to him. "She can do things we can't. Together we are stronger."

Stratton sits back from his trough and puts a leg on the couch. "Did I give you permission to call me that?"

"I'll call you whatever I want, Jace. Know your place."

This mild-mannered and soft spoken girl has a higher position with the Society. I did not see that coming. Her vibrant red hair, cut in a straight bob, gently tickles her collarbone. A narrow jawline enhances her cold-as-ice vibe. It doesn't match with her casual movements. It's like she could care less about anyone, but also hate everyone at the same time.

"Whatever." Stratton shrugs. "Bond away, Neira."

"I will."

Neira crosses her legs, adjusting her jeans. She points at the lounge chair opposite of hers.

"Please," she insists and directs me with her eyes.

"No, I'm good," I huff. "I'll stand."

"Fine, that's fine. I want to take this time to properly introduce myself." She looks back out the window.

"Ok, whatever," I say.

"Why don't you start with your Push ability," Stratton interrupts.

"Why don't you shut up and do what you're told, Jace." She throws a vicious stare his way. Her eyes cold as stone.

"Have fun with that, Princess." he grins, returning to the dessert platter.

I turn back to Neira who's locked on me. She has that same overly calm vibe that Jax has, but her calmness is fueled by something darker.

"Your parents recruited me from the Rauner Trust," Neira says. "The Trust controlled the Montana region. My ability was being wasted there. Greedy men using me to expand territory was getting annoying."

I've never heard of this sector group. Amanda and I have never traveled that far north. The Magnus Order's borders blocked most roads in that direction. And there's no way we would go further east. It's far too barbaric in the great plains.

"It was about four months ago when I left," Neira continues. "When I came to this city, I found your mom. She welcomed me with open arms. She's a great leader. She inspires me."

"And how did you so easily find Laney?" Stratton prods her.

For some reason, Stratton is resentful of Neira. He takes every chance he gets to poke at her. Maybe he's jealous of her rank or maybe she's closer to Laney than he is. I'm not sure.

"Oh, Jace," she sighs. If you weren't such a good tool for the Society, I would..."

"You'd what?" He demands, staring her down this time.

She ignores him, taking a deep breath followed by a slow exhale. When she turns back to me, I almost see a crack in her unbreakable exterior.

"Where were we?" She grins.

"No, I'd like to know about your ability, actually." I rest my hand on the lounge chair across from her.

"Ok, sure." Her smile wavers. "Well, I have the ability to instantly counter any push from other Influencers. I can defuse anyone from messing with the reality that surrounds me. It comes in handy when I need to move between sectors."

Now it makes sense. Jax tried over and over to manipulate the Harvester wall outside this building. Every time he tried, his Push would fizzle out. Like it never fully formed.

"So, that's why you've been shadowing us?" I ask. "Just in case we don't play by the Society's rules."

"That's just the half of it." Stratton mouth curls into a sneer. "Don't forget the little thing about turning the unevolved into temporary Influencers."

"Stratton," she snarls. "Enough already!"

I take a step back toward the door. My natural instinct to find safety kicks in. My mind flickers to thoughts of Farren.

"You can turn normal people into Influencers?" I ask, pacing a few steps back and forth. "How is this possible? What does that mean?"

"Yes, I can unlock their simple minds and give them a glimpse of the connection they normally can't access."

"I still don't understand." I raise my palms and shrug.

"You're thinking too much about the world our mind creates for us. Reality is just our brain interpreting all the waves and signals that bombard us at every second. What you feel is not solid, it's your mind's way of making sense of things. So, knowing that, we're all just a lump of atoms and particles. I'm just able to pick at them like a bag of marbles."

"The Society's own personal god," Stratton says to me.

"That's not right." I shake my head. "It's bad enough Influencers meddle in the moods of others, but what you do is... is..."

"It's evolution." She cuts me off. "It's how we save humanity. It's how we heal this country—this world."

"So, you just enlighten people with a glimpse of our ability and yank it away? What's the point of that?"

Neira comes to her feet. "You don't get it. If I awaken them for just a moment, they become far easier to guide. Their awareness is not closed in anymore. It's awakened and far easier to access for Influencers with your special kind of talent."

Grabbing hold of the consciousness of people like Amanda and others who've accepted how reality works is effortless. The reality they connect to is much greater than the closed minds of those who don't understand. Neira opening up people's awareness creates a potential cascade of manipulation. Like a daisy chain of control.

"You see, Kaylin..." Stratton pauses, wiping the chocolate from the corners of his mouth with his sleeve. "... we're *much* better weapons with little ol' Neira around."

"Let's give Kaylin a chance to rest." Neira looks to Stratton. "She's going to need it."

Stratton rolls his eyes, pulling himself off the couch. Neira nods as she walks past me. My eyes pan down and I stare at the wear and smudges on my boots.

"Have a *fantastic* night, Kaylin," Stratton says, thudding his way to the door.

With a lock of the door, I'm once again alone. Amanda's probably sweeping Magnus hubs with Farren and the others in the mountains. My newly discovered brother, Jax, is, I don't know, somewhere. I'm no closer to my extremely disconnected, warmongering parents either. Here I am, in a luxury suite staring out a sprawling expanse of glass, watching the sun inch closer to the tops of the skyscrapers on the horizon. The only place I want to be now is wandering Lost Souls with Amanda. Hiding and most likely starving, but it's familiar. Not like this. Not like the void of direction I'm living in now.

6

FAMILY HISTORY

THERE'S NO RESTING for me. I'm not going to pretend I'm on vacation here. I need answers. The only ones with answers are my so-called parents. It's time for another heart to heart.

I jiggle the handle on my door, partially thinking it might be locked from the outside. To my surprise, it opens. The hall is empty. No hulking guards in lame trench coats. Just the surveillance cameras above with their red blinking lights.

The silence is eerie as I walk down this empty hall toward the elevator. No workers or other *special* guests anywhere. I reach the end where the elevator is. I press the button but nothing happens. It doesn't light up or ding. A few more taps and still nothing. Maybe the generator that feeds power to it is off. I'll stretch my legs and take the stairs instead.

I cross back over this long corridor to the far end. A glowing green LED sign reads 'exit' above a steel door. I press the long, horizontal bar in the middle of the door, but it doesn't budge. They've locked it. The steady rhythm of my heartbeat jumps to a faster pace. I turn and rush to the stairwell at the other end of this level. My feet shake the ground as I stomp through, making quick work of the distance. I rapidly press the lever and grunt. Locked. I guess I'm not as special as I thought.

I peer over my shoulder and look at the doors that line each side of the hall. Back and forth, I check each one as I head back to my room. No luck.

I reach my door and hope I'm not locked out of it too. Luckily, it opens. Rushing in, I'm stopped in my tracks.

"Hi Kaylin," Laney says, sitting in the lounge chair across from the one Neira used.

Relic walks into the open room from the direction of my bedroom and nods at me.

"Wait, how did you get here so fast?" I ask, looking at Laney.

"We were on our way to see you, my dear."

Seems like a strange coincidence that I was just leaving to see her, but whatever. I need answers before I go crazy. I fold my arms as I move into the middle of the room and stand a few feet from where she sits.

"Am I a prisoner?" I ask "Why can't I leave this floor?"

Relic moves next to Laney, resting a hand on the back of her chair. His coat slips open for a split second, once again revealing the pistol strapped to his waist.

"You're new here," he says. "We didn't become the biggest organization by trusting everyone."

"So, my own mother doesn't trust me?" I shift my eyes to Laney.

"Kaylin, I want to trust you. I do. But you've been gone for so long."

"Whose fault is that?" I snarl.

"You don't know what you're talking about, Kaylin." Laney leans forward. "You have no idea how hard that was. You come from a strong Influencer gene pool. We couldn't let you get into the wrong hands. We were right to hide you. Your power is terrifying."

"You're afraid of me?" I ask.

"No, no." She sits back again and crosses her legs. "That's not what I meant. If they took you, you would have been a weapon for terror."

My hands drop to my sides. "And I'm not just going to be a weapon for you?"

Laney stands and turns to look out the window. It gets dark fast here. I feel like I've missed the whole day.

"You remind me so much of your Aunt Leeyah," Laney says, shaking her head. "She fought everything I said. Thought she knew everything. But in the end her ability was used to help take down this world. I'm trying to save you from that."

"No one uses me, no one."

The room goes quiet. Relic taps on the wood lining the lounge chair as he looks to Laney. She continues to stare out the window.

"Kaylin," Laney says softly. "You're home now. Your family is together. Don't mess this up, please."

I don't dare ask her what she worries I'll mess up. This *beautiful* family reunion or her war plans.

"Where's Jax?" I ask.

"He needed to get away for a bit," Relic says. "He'll come around."

"I want to see him. Where is he?"

"Just give him time, Kaylin," Laney says. "This has not been easy for him. We'll all have a nice breakfast in the morning, ok?"

She leads Relic out of my room, only offering me a forced smile as she closes the door behind herself.

My heart races as the door clanks shut. I want to open it and follow them out—get off this floor—but they already don't trust me. I need to be smart.

It's strange how I get to stay another night in a luxury suite with all my needs taken care of, but all I can think of is how I miss what I left behind. It was hard and I was often hungry, but I had Amanda. And then there's Farren. I miss them.

I pace in front of the window for a few minutes, unease filling my mind. It's late afternoon, they'll be bringing dinner soon. Maybe I can find a way out when they come.

Jax enters my thoughts. Where is he? I can't leave here without him. I wish I knew what he was thinking. He's not one to join another power-hungry sector group, but these are his parents. Well, mine too. A rapid thud on the door snaps me back to attention.

I'm not ready for another pep talk from *mother dearest*. I hope it's not her again. They must just be serving dinner early tonight.

Whack-whack-whack.

"Geez, hold on," I shout.

Pulling the door open, I see Jax panting heavily as he leans on the wall just to the side.

"Jax? There you are. Where have you been?"

He lumbers in as I move to the side. I pop my head out the suite and look down the hall in both directions. He's alone.

"I'm sorry Kaylin." He wraps me up in a soft hug. "I'm sorry I left you alone here. I just needed to get away and think."

"How did you get here? Do you have access to the building?"

He pulls away and looks up to the camera in the corner above the door. With his head, he gestures toward the bathroom. He takes my hand and leads me down the short hall off the kitchen area. We file into the marble lined bathroom and he closes the door behind us.

"They don't have surveillance in here," he says.

"What's going on?" I ask. "Are you alright?"

He leans up against the smooth white counter top. His head sinks a bit.

"This is too much for me. It's Mom and Dad. I've thought of this moment every day for the last few years. I thought I would find them and be done with this life of war and manipulation."

I sit next to him and rest my head on his shoulder. "I know what you mean. It doesn't feel right. What are we going to do?"

"I can't leave them. They might be different, but they're still our parents. I feel stuck."

I lift my head and stare at the back of the closed door. He's not ready to leave, but I am.

"I can't stay." I turn to him, unable to look into his eyes. "I'm sorry, nothing feels right about this."

A deep sigh leaves his chest and he stands to face me. "Please don't leave me alone. I need you."

The familiar thud on the front door rattles the bathroom door. Dinner time I guess. Jax and I aren't done with this conversation.

"We better answer them or they're going to think I jumped out a window." I rest a hand on his forearm and smile.

"Knowing you... you just might." He laughs.

We make our way to the door. Jax sits on the couch. I guess he's staying for dinner. I'm glad. As soon as I unlock the latch, a deep boom explodes, shaking the window in the living area. A subtle vibration trickles below my feet. I pull the door open as I fall back. The dinner tray lays on the ground and the two servers jump to their feet and fly down the hall.

"Kaylin!" Jax shouts. "Are you alright?"

He rushes up to me, grabbing my shoulders, trying to catch my eyes.

"I'm fine, I'm fine. What was that?"

"We must be under attack," he says.

"By who?"

Jax pokes his head out the door. "I'm not sure, but we better move."

He grabs my hand and leads me into the hall, we step over food from the toppled over cart. A new explosion shakes the building. The suite doors thrash in their frames. That was much closer than the last. We pick up our pace and reach the stairwell door. It was left open by the fleeing Society staff.

"What's your plan?" I ask, breathing heavier now.

"I don't know, but being up this high is not smart."

"Let's head down and go from there," I suggest.

"Sounds good."

All we hear are our pattering footsteps as we fly down each flight, a soft red haze pulsates as it brightens our way. Feels like we are descending forever. No sign of the servers or any one from the Society. We reached the bottom floor and face a metal door.

"That's the door to the lobby," Jax says, hunched over.

I pull on the handle, but the door doesn't move. I turn to see a red blinking light on the key panel just to the right. "It's locked, now what?"

He reaches into the pocket of his dark jeans and pulls out a white card. "We use this."

I narrow my eyes on him. "So, I guess mommy and daddy trust you?"

"First born privileges." He raises his eyebrows in amusement.

The panel beeps and turns to a soft green as the door clicks.

He cracks it open slowly, resting his shoulder against the frame. He stares into the lobby for a moment before returning his gaze to me.

"Relic's in there manning the door with several guards," he says.

"Please help me get out," I beg. "I don't want to be here anymore."

He bites his lower lip before exhaling slowly. "I will get you out, but I can't leave. Not yet at least. Not until I know more."

"I understand."

I don't have time to think about leaving him here. Getting out of this chaos is dominating my mind.

"I feel plenty of Harvesters out there," he says, his eyes closed now. "I'm going to move them close. You need to get them to draw the Society around the building. Hopefully Neira is not paying attention."

If he pulls them close, I can Push them to rush the back of the building. Hopefully the Society will follow.

Muffled cracks of gunfire start drowning out the commands Relic is shouting. The Harvesters are closing in. It's my turn. Jax confirms by resting a hand on my shoulder.

My eyes close and my breathing slows. Sounds fade the deeper I go into my Push. Desperation fills my mind as I connect to a large collection of men and women just outside. I tug at their desires and push out thoughts of abundance and opportunity near the back of the building. A primal need for *more* takes hold of them. This amplifies their existing greedy tendencies. My Push takes hold as I feel an emotional shift in their collective thoughts.

"We're good," I say to Jax. "They should be moving now."

He once again peaks out the barely open exit door. Pulling back, he looks at me and nods.

"They took the bait, let's move."

A tightness in my chest makes me hesitate, but Jax takes my hand and pulls me through the now fully open door. We run through the fancy lobby, our feet smacking down on the elegant tile beneath us. The main lobby doors come into view. We're almost out.

"Jax!" a voice shouts from down the hall near the exit.

I turn and see Laney running to us with several armed guards as well as Neira at her side.

"Hold right there," a stocky armed man commands as the rest meet us in front of the glass doors leading out.

Jax stops cold in his tracks, forcing me to slam into his back.

"Where do you two think you're going?" Laney demands, staring right at Jax.

Five guards raise guns at us now. Laney folds her arms, breathing deeply as she tries to catch her breath.

"Mom," Jax says. "I'm taking Kaylin out of here. She wants to go."

"Go? Go where?" She turns to me. "Your family is here. Your life is here. There's nowhere *to* go."

"That's my choice," I say. "Family doesn't hold each other hostage."

"Just let her go, Mom," Jax pleads. "You can't force her into your life. She has to find her own path."

"But I can and I will," Laney says, her brows furrowed. "If she's not with the cause, then she's against our family."

My mouth drops open and a cool sensation lines my core. My so-called mother is no better than any of the other sector bosses.

I open my Push to the people outside, looking for some help, but this time when I connect to one, my ability fails to grab hold of their awareness. Neira. She's on to us now.

"Please, just let me go. I don't belong here. I'm not fighting this war for you."

"Guards, take her to the holding wing," Laney commands. "Looks like she needs to learn some respect."

"Mom," Jax snarls. "Stop this. I'll stay, but you have to let her go."

"Move out of the way, son. Kaylin has to earn her way into our family. I gave her a chance. Now, she's going to start at the bottom."

A discharge rattles just outside the doors before the glass shatters, throwing shards everywhere. Bullets zip pass us and pelt the guards closest to Jax and I. Laney and the remaining men fall back deeper into the connecting corridor inside the lobby. Jax wraps me up and we fall to the ground, shielding our heads. My ears ring as the gunfire draws closer. I slide on my side and Jax follows. We make it behind a couch and press our backs firmly against it. Laney and her guards are nowhere in sight now.

Several people race into the opening just in front of us. They're in full armor. Dark grey plating covers most of their body and tinted helmets cover their heads. Scanning the lobby, the tallest of them spots us and signals the others. They are not Harvesters.

"It's them," a muffled voice sounds from under the helmet.

With both knees planted, Jax kneels in front of me ready to leap at them when one of the armored fighters raises a hand, signaling for the rest to lower their weapons. The fighter pulls the helmet off. It's a woman. She has greying hair and a soft expression. Her face is relaxed and I don't sense she wants to hurt us. A smile inches up and fills her face.

"Kaylin, is that you?"

"What?" is all I can say. "Stay back," Jax says to the woman.

"Oh, I'm sorry. We're not going to hurt you."

"Why are you attacking us?" Jax asks, rising to one knee, ready to protect me.

"This is not an attack," the woman insists. "This is a rescue mission."

Two of the heavily armored men fan out and take cover on the rear wall that leads into the building. Their rifles butted against their shoulders.

"Did you come for us?" I ask. "How do you know my name?"

"Because I gave it to you."

7

AWAKENING

THIS MAKES NO sense. My eyes narrow and I analyze everything about the woman—her dull blue eyes, the shoulder length haircut, and that smile she can't stop.

"What are you talking about?" I ask.

"Let's get you safe first and I'll fill you in on everything after," she says.

I really have no other options—rot with the Society, or take a chance with this person?

I place a hand on Jax's shoulder. He turns to me, eyes relaying the agony his heart must be feeling.

"Please come with me," I beg.

He looks down the empty hall where his mother fled and turns back to me with a single nod. I'm the first up, and I offer him a hand, which I'm so glad he accepts. The woman signals for everyone to leave the building.

Without another word, we follow her, trailing a few feet behind her and her guards as they guide us through the shattered opening and into the darkened streets of Seattle. Fighters with the same riot gear are posted at every corner the deeper we head into the city. Gunfire eases, eventually stopping completely as we're led into an abandoned hyperloop terminal to rest.

The woman orders her fighters to secure all corners of the structure. Jax and I find an old service vehicle and sit in the bed, trying to catch our breaths. Alone for a moment, Jax slides closer to me. "I don't know who this woman is, but be careful with her."

"After what I've gone through the last few days? I'm not trusting anyone."

The woman walks up to us, unclasping her body armor. "Ah, that's better," she sighs, resting the gear on a counter to the side of where we sit.

"Who are you?" I ask, not waiting for any small talk.

"My name is Leeyah," she says, her smile no longer there, "and I have a feeling you guys might've heard of me?"

"You're Leeyah? *Aunt* Leeyah?" Jax asks her.

Her head dips as she avoids our eyes. I straighten up, waiting for her to respond.

"Yes, my name is Leeyah, and I am your Aunt," she says to Jax before turning to me. "But I'm not your Aunt, Kaylin."

"I don't understand," I say. "Are you saying Jax is not my brother?"

"No, he's not. He's your cousin."

My stomach tightens and I slide off the truck to my feet. Folding my arms over my chest, I take a step away from her. She stays put, but keeps her eyes locked on me.

"What are you talking about?" Jax asks. "This doesn't make sense. Our mother—"

"Your mom lied to you," she cuts Jax off. "She lied to both of you. We have someone on the inside."

"So…I'm *your* daughter?" the words barely escape from my lips.

She walks up to me, reaching out to take my hand. I pull back, keeping my arms folded. She drops her arms to her side and takes a step back.

"Yes, Kaylin. I'm your mother. You have no idea how long I've been waiting to see you again."

"I don't understand any of this," I say, shaken to my core. "How can I believe you?"

"She's right." Jax jumps out of the truck and steps to my side. "My mom told me about you, about what you did to start all of this."

She looks at him, shaking her head. "Jax, she's lying to you. To you both. Your mom is angry, and has been for a long time."

"Angry at what?" I ask.

Leeyah paces a few steps before stopping in front of a fogged-up window that looks out onto the street.

"My sister was my best friend. She watched out for me when we were younger. But as soon as my ability showed, she became afraid of me. She became obsessed with 'curing' me. I was younger than you, Kaylin, when she and I had our falling out."

"I don't care about any of this." My voice shakes and my breathing elevates to match my pounding heart. "If you're my mom, then tell me where you've been my entire life. Why did you abandon me?"

She pivots, quickly meeting my steely gaze. She moves forward, only stopped by the animosity resting behind my eyes.

"I *never* abandoned you," she insists, her eyes welling up. "She took you from me. Laney stole you."

"That's ridiculous," Jax snaps. "She would never."

A gasp escapes me, as if my soul was twisted inside. My vision blurs from the stinging tears that have bubbled to the surface. Not wanting anyone to see, I crane my head to the side and quickly wipe them away with my sleeve.

"I'm sorry," she says to Jax. "She's not the same person you remember. She's been fighting her inner demons ever since the world started to collapse. She took my Kaylin to protect you."

"What are you talking about?" I ask.

"The sector groups were searching for me for years before either of you were born. This was about the time they started abusing Influencers for their power-hungry purposes. They wanted me. They wanted my genetics. If they got a hold of me, they hoped to produce children with the Push ability. I was able to hide from them, but they knew who Laney was—*where* she was. That would have to do."

She leans back against the window. Cracks in the clouds allow sunlight to filter into the smudged-up glass, creating a halo around her. "Laney was not about to lose Jax or be forced to give up a second child. I stayed close to her, hoping one day we could be like we were when we were young. She knew I gave birth to you, Kaylin. I never saw her or you again."

I pace a few feet from her now, thoughts running rampant. *Can it be true? Is this my real mother?* I've been thrown from one lie to another over the last couple of days. My trust in people is gone.

"You're saying she stole me from you and then had a change of heart?" I ask, grasping for answers. "Why didn't she just give me back to you?"

"There must be some good left in her, but she must've been able to face me after what she did. She didn't change the name I gave you, though. Maybe she wanted me to find you. Or maybe she had this plan to bring you into her war all along. I just don't know."

"Why didn't you stop her from taking me then?" I ask. "How could you let that happen?"

"It was the worst day of my life. I couldn't—"

"I don't buy this," Jax interrupts before he turns and walks toward the exit.

"Jax, please don't go," I plead, reaching out for him.

"I need to think. This is too much."

He walks out of the terminal and disappears down a back alley out of my sight. I want to go with him, but my emotions are split in two. I need to figure this out.

"Why should I believe any of this?" I ask, turning back to her.

"Kaylin, feel inside," Leeyah insists. "You can sense who I am. Influencers' abilities are far greater than you know."

"What does that mean?" I ask, furrowing my brow.

"Calm your body and mind. Find the stream of reality that binds us all. That bond works between Influencers, too. Once you find the common link between all humans, you will find a familiar feeling that only family has. Please try."

I've always had a sense of people near me, but I have no idea what a family bond should feel like.

"How would you feel any different then Jax, or even Laney? They're family too, *supposedly*."

"It's not the same," she says. "If he was actually your brother, you would have eventually felt the difference. Immediate family just feels different."

She calls one of the guards that's milling about at the far end of the room. He struts over.

"Sense Nance here," she insists, pulling on his arm to bring him closer. "Notice how his awareness is familiar. I bet you're so used to the way people feel now that you're blind to it. Then, try me."

Pausing, I just stare at the man. I don't really want to get caught up in anymore lies. I sigh, but decide to amuse her for now.

I open up my awareness to my surroundings and let the conscious imprints of everyone nearby trickle into my mind. The man feels like a shadow has just fallen over me. I know it's there, but I don't think anything more of it. It's just there.

Shifting my attention to Leeyah, there's an instant wash of warmth that creates the illusion of a tingly sensation on my skin. If I actually focus on my skin, it's not really there. My mind's just interpreting her awareness in this way. Then a sense of ease and overwhelming comfort floods me. It's beautiful.

"You can understand how I feel now," Leeyah says, breaking me from the connection. "I opened my awareness to you the minute I saw you. I didn't need to try to feel you—you just consumed me."

"How do I know you're not just doing this to me somehow?" I ask, taking a step back from her. "What's her name, Neira, with the Society, can alter an Influencer's Push. You could be trying to trick me."

She instructs the man to leave the room. We're alone now. She walks up to me and takes my wrists. I pull back just a bit, but let her hold on.

"You know who I am, Kaylin. A mother never forgets her child, and a child will always have a connection with her mother as well."

My chin starts to quiver and my eyes start to well up. I know who she is, and I want to hate her for losing me, but I can't. I lower my head and bury it into her shoulder. She releases my wrists and wraps her warm arms around me, pulling me in closer. The tears flow now, and the weight of the world releases from me. Only her embrace tethers me to this moment.

8

DISRUPTED

THE BUILDING SHAKES, breaking me from my mother's arms. Dust falls from the old, brittle ceiling, fluttering onto our heads. I pull back and look at Leeyah. She stands still, shifting her eyes to both sides as she studies what's going on.

"We're under attack," she says, spinning on her heels to face the exit. "We need to move."

"I need to find Jax," I plead.

"We will, I promise."

Leeyah grabs my arm and guides me to the open hyperloop hatch. Peering out, she calls to her team. One by one they signal each other and fall back to us. There's pops of gunfire in the distance as Leeyah's small group of four boys and two girls reach us, the constant rattle getting closer.

"We're all accounted for, Ma'am," a skinny kid with long, light blonde hair streaming out of his beanie says.

"It's the Society," one of the girls reports. "Stratton and Neira are leading them."

Leeyah reaches down for her helmet and without asking shoves it on my head. I instinctively grasp at it, but she puts her hands on mine, holding it on me.

"I need you safe. I just got you back. Please wear this."

I don't resist, but leaving her exposed doesn't make me feel good. From what I can tell, though, she's more than capable of handling herself.

"They've cut off our route to the camp," the short, stocky girl says. "We're going to need to fall back deeper into the city."

"I don't like this, Breece," Leeyah says, her hand resting on the girl's arm.

"What about Jax?" I ask with more urgency this time.

"He's very capable," Leeyah tells me. "We're not leaving him. We just need to find a more secure location. Once things settle down, I'll have my team bring him back."

Her eyes lock on mine, her brow lifting just slightly. There's a warmth in her gaze. I *want* to trust her. I can't go rushing into the raging battle after Jax. All I can do at this moment is nod to Leeyah.

"Let's move," Leeyah orders her team. "Eric, Jen, Orren, head east and try to get back to the headquarters. The rest of us will go wide to throw them off."

Everyone jumps into motion, gathering their supplies and weapons.

Leeyah turns back to me. "Stay behind me."

We slide against the hyperloop's outer wall as we race toward the darkened inner alleyways, hoping to gain some distance from those coming for us. Breece darts out in front. She's much faster than she looks. Leeyah's close behind, constantly looking over her shoulder to check on me. The other two guys hang back, providing a buffer for us in the front.

Alley after alley starts to look the same. They all have little lighting with dampened, narrow corridors. Trash is piled up everywhere, the scent of rotten waste unrelenting. Leeyah calls for the skinny blonde boy to take the lead. He carries a much larger rifle then the rest.

"Gareth, take a wider angle," Leeyah orders. "I'm sure we're not alone."

Not alone? She means the Harvesters. In the chaos, I completely forgot to keep my awareness open. I need to help. It's hard as we run from Society fighters, but I'm still able to expand my sense of the area. Life is teaming everywhere in this maze of concrete and asphalt. A subtle presence hovers around me from all angles, just out of reach.

The alley opens up to a street around the next bend. Old, beat-up cars cram the opening, funneling us into a focal point. A large gathering enters my mind. I slow, but it's too late. Gareth sprints through the chokepoint.

"Stop!" I yell.

A blur of something swings from around the corner, cracking Gareth in the head, his helmet flies several yards. A large man pulls a metal bat back down to his side, a grin filling his face. Leeyah comes to a quick stop, a pistol in one hand and a fist up on the opposite side. Breece stops just before batting practice. Gareth is crumpled over, blood covering his face as he lays in a dirty pool of runoff water in the gutter.

Flanked by several men and a couple of women in the rear, the man with the bat tightens his grip, his muscles bursting from his sleeveless jacket. Leeyah points her gun at him, but the three men realign their rifles on her.

The bald man with tattoos covering his smooth scalp raises his bat. "Looks like my trap caught us something real nice," he snarls. "We have you covered from all sides. Drop your weapons. Now."

Scanning the setting, I can't see a way out, only back where we came from. That's not an option, as the Society's not far behind. We can't leave Gareth, either. I can still feel his consciousness; he's not dead.

"You don't want to be here right now," Leeyah says to the man. "The Vernon Society is close. They're not as lenient as I'll be."

The man hoots, followed by what seems like forced laughter from the rest. "I *own* these streets," he boasts. "I don't fear nobody."

I'm about to use my Push to make these Harvesters flee when I sense it. The muddling of consciousness. A deep sense of unease and sadness washes over me.

Stratton.

Before I can counter it, blasts from the street rattle me back to the current moment. The Harvesters mow each other down. Pops of light fill the air as limbs snap back, blood spraying everywhere. The constant barrage of gunfire forces me to cover my head and crouch down. I peek up to find Leeyah and the rest of our team have taken cover behind a burnt-out car up in front of me. Leeyah's confused at why I didn't follow, but they know what to do in an attack. They flank Leeyah, keeping their focus on Gareth.

The shots slow, and one by one the Harvesters fall, blood dripping from countless bullet wounds. I will never get used to seeing people die like this.

"Kaylin!" Leeyah calls from up ahead. "We have to go! I can't protect them much longer!"

Protect who? What does she mean? I look over my shoulder and take a deep breath before rushing to her and the others. As soon as I reach her, the small group surrounds me, protecting me from all sides.

"Nance, go get Gareth," Leeyah says before turning to me. "Kaylin, can you watch their consciousness?"

"Um, yeah, okay," I say. "Stratton did this. He does horrible things. I can block him, but there's another one that can counter my Push."

"I know," she says, taking my hand. "I know all about the Society's people—her people."

I almost forgot for a moment that her sister, my aunt, is the delusional leader of the Vernon Society.

Leeyah releases my hand and turns to Breece to say something, but I tune them out, opening my awareness as far as I possibly can. Shadows creep all around me as the subtle essence of life trickles into my mind. Stratton's wicked brand of Push ability is nowhere to be found.

Nance startles me as he drags an unconscious Gareth back to our position. He holds a torn-off sleeve from his shirt against Gareth's head. I close my eyes to refocus my ability when everything stops and all the life swirling around my mind vanishes. My ability is gone. Neira's close.

"She's here," I call out. "Neira's stopped my Push."

"Mine too," Leeyah says. "We need to move."

Hers too? Leeyah's ability is still active? An Influencer's ability never works at her age, but I don't have time to ask about it. Heavy footsteps thrum from down the street, every *thud* rattling my core.

"We need to go!" Breece calls out.

We creep out from the cover of the car and head toward the street where the Harvesters lie dead. Tiptoeing over them, I avoid looking down as much as possible.

"Hurry, Kaylin," Nance pleads.

I'm stopped dead in my tracks as a heavy lull washes over me, my body tensing up. That familiar, dark sense of dread trickles before my awareness. Stratton is near, and my Push ability is severed. My skin crawls with fear. I'm useless because of Neira.

"It's too late," I plead to Leeyah. "They have us."

9

SEVERED

LEEYAH LOOKS DEFEATED. Her face tenses as fear grips her, her jaw locking tight. Stratton's brand of amplified depression is filling the area, surrounding us as well.

"No," I breathe.

A slow rumble fills every alley. I crane my head in all directions, trying to reconnect to the collective consciousness of the moment. Nothing. I'm simply ordinary. Even my sense of Stratton's ability trickles away, leaving me alone with my own thoughts and emotions.

"Fall back to the car," Leeyah says. "Nance, Breece, cover opposite directions."

The rumble turns into thunder. We crouch and make our way back to the false safety of the beat-up car. Rust has nearly consumed every inch of its metal frame. Leeyah grabs my arms and guides me to lean against the side between her and the rest of our team, but it's no use. We have nowhere to go.

The dimly lit road only enhances my growing anxiety. If the nearly full moon wasn't overhead, it would be pitch-black, and even then, clouds threaten to conceal our false sense of security.

"We'll need to shoot our way out," Breece insists. "As soon as we get a target, we need to open fire and head in the opposite direction."

Seconds later, Harvesters pour out from every street and around every building. Their heavy footfalls become uniform, like the heart beat of the city ripping from its chest.

"Oh no," I mutter. "We're surrounded."

A few yards out, the filthy, deviant flood of Harvesters comes to a complete stop. With lifeless eyes, they look past us, their faces void of emotion. No doubt this is Stratton's handiwork.

"There is zero chance you have enough bullets to take them all down," a familiar voice calls from a distance. "Lower your weapons."

Stratton.

I turn to Leeyah, her face etched with worry. Her eyes race back and forth before she looks at Nance and Breece and nods. Nance purses his lips, a scowl overtaking them. He doesn't want to give up.

"Nance, *now!*" Leeyah orders.

He scoffs, but drops the weapon to the ground and kicks it away. Breece does the same, then returns her attention to the unconscious Gareth, pressing the blood-soaked cloth against his head.

"Listen," Leeyah whispers loud enough for us to hear, "we're not done here. I didn't find my daughter just to lose her now. They would have killed us by now if they were going to. Wait for my lead."

We all nod and return our gaze to the hoard encircling us. My hands shake, but I keep them close to my body. This sense of helplessness is unsettling.

There's movement down the street we came from. Harvesters step to the side, creating an opening in the crowd. I glance back to Leeyah, but she calmly shakes her head. Returning my focus to the movement, I take a deep breath and exhale, steadying myself.

Six men emerge in body armor similar to what Leeyah's team is wearing. They all wear Society trench coats over their armor. The beanies look ridiculous over their helmets, but somehow that makes them even more terrifying.

They inch forward and fan out, large rifles trained on us. Two silhouettes approach from behind them, coming into focus as they strut closer. That trademark smirk fills Stratton's face while Neira remains poised and confident. Her chin inches up as she interlocks her fingers in front of her waist.

"Leeyah, nice to see you again," Neira says. "I wish it wasn't under these circumstances, though."

Leeyah stands and folds her arms. "These are the exact circumstances you and that *creature* created for us. Don't kid yourself."

Stratton huffs and shakes his head. It's almost as if that comment hurt his feelings—if he had any to hurt.

"I guess that's true." Neira nods. "But don't you think your constant meddling in the Society's business warranted this action? And then you go and take Kaylin from Laney."

"She is *my* daughter, not hers," Leeyah snaps.

"I'm not here to discuss family matters. I'm here to bring an end to this."

Leeyah steps out a few feet in front of us. The armed men tighten their grips on their rifles, shifting their shoulders forward.

"So, this is it?" Leeyah pleads. "You're just going to let these goons mow us down in cold blood?"

Neira chuckles softly. "Oh, no, that wouldn't be fun. I'm going to let the Harvesters do our dirty work."

I look from side to side at the army surrounding us. There must be at least a hundred of them jammed into this area. My breathing picks up as fear builds in my chest. I try again to use my ability, but nothing happens. It's like there's a dull void around me.

"Is this really who you are, Stratton?" I ask, grasping at straws. "Do you have no conscious of your own?"

Stratton narrows his eyes on me, barely moving his head. "I do what's best for me, nothing more."

"And *this* is what's best for you? Murdering people without a second thought?"

His glare softens a fraction before the determination in his eyes return. "I have not murdered anyone. I've never laid a finger on anyone in my life. There's no blood on my hands."

"Keep telling yourself that," I snarl. "You're a monster."

"Stratton?" Neira interrupts. "Can we do this already? I'm tired, and Ray is making broiled lobster tails for dinner tonight."

The guards snicker at her comment. The amount of heartlessness in this world astounds me.

"Let Kaylin live," Leeyah begs. "You can't tell me Laney wants this for her."

"She's worn out her welcome," Neira replies.

Leeyah grits her teeth before turning back to me. She comes to my side and wraps her arms around me, squeezing me tightly. "I'm sorry I didn't get a chance to know you better. You stay behind me. They're going to have to go through me first."

Her words hit me hard. Before this moment, I was too distracted to let my emotions truly soak in. This is my *mother*. Not even having a chance to sit down and talk with her is a cruel joke. I'm not going to stand by and let them wipe her out just so I can be the last to die.

I grab Leeyah's arms and pull them off me. I look into her eyes before turning to face them, readying my stance. Stratton shakes his head at me as if I'm foolish. His eyes shut and a moment later the crowd stirs, inching closer to us. My stomach drops as the realization of what's going to happen sinks in.

Painfully slow, the hoard of Harvesters lurch forward, their dirty faces void of life as they move in. Our helpless group falls back into a tighter circle.

The first line reaches us. Several teenage boys charge us with nothing more than the amplified rage Stratton's toying with. Breece thrusts her boot into one of the taller boy's kneecaps, dropping him to the ground. The boy's high-pitched scream reminds me that these are just kids.

Not wanting to hurt anyone, I try one more time to force my Push onto the gathering, but my concentration is aimless. There's nothing to grab onto.

Nance drives his head forward into another boy's temple, and there's a sickening *thud* as it connects. The boy spins, releasing a guttural yell as he plows into another Harvester. A heavy-set woman and a bulky man grab Leeyah's arms, wrenching her from our group. I claw at the man, drawing blood as I scratch down the length of his forearms. He releases her and I pull her back behind me, then ball up my fist and punch the woman in the side of the head, my knuckles bursting into throbbing pain. I draw my hand in close to my chest, trying to smother the intense fire pulsing up my arm now. The woman I hit staggers back, releasing my mother.

Leeyah returns to the false protection of our cluster as more and more people pile in, knocking into one another, all trying to get their hands on us. An ocean of people flood the street, heads bobbing like waves in a storm as they fight to reach us. Breece disappears as Harvesters tackle her, smothering her. Fear forces me to close my eyes.

This is it. This is where I die.
Then I feel it.

10

A BOND

MY EYES FLASH open. His awareness washes over the entire block.

Jax.

The Harvesters stop. Slowly, they turn, looking to leave. The zombie-like groans and hate-filled faces are replaced with calmness. The crowd disperses and the mob trickles out of the street into the alleys and side roads.

He came back. I knew Jax wouldn't leave me. I pivot from side to side looking for him, but he's nowhere. It's too dark to see beyond this street.

"Kaylin, are you alright?" Leeyah asks, resting a hand on my shoulder.

"Yeah, I'm fine."

"We really need to move now," Breece insists, staggering back to her feet. Cuts and scrapes cover her face and arms.

"Right, let's go before the Society can sort through the crowd," Leeyah urges.

Crack, crack, crack!

We flinch and crouch down as flashes brighten the street up ahead. The Society guards are firing on the crowd. People cry out in agony as the chaos grows. We need to move or we're next—again.

Gareth has come to and is able to walk on his own. He wraps his arm across Nance's shoulder, staggering a bit. Gareth was lucky. He was protected behind us during the madness.

Nance points to the bend where Gareth was assaulted. "This way," he says.

We form a line, pushing our way through the scattering crowd. The Harvesters have no interest in us. They seem to just want to leave. Jax's ability is truly amazing. He can affect so many so quickly. I want to find him, but we need to find a safe place away from the armed men.

More gunfire blares in the background as we pull further away from them. We're able to run now as the cluster of manipulated Harvesters thins. My heart wants to beat out of my chest. I'm not built for sprinting long distances, amazed at how Leeyah and the rest can charge ahead. They have to be running on fumes.

It's been five minutes and my legs can't take anymore. Luckily, Leeyah raises her hand, signaling us to stop. Hunched over, trying to catch her breath, Leeyah peers up at Nance, panting out, "We need... to find a way... out of here. This place... is going to be... crawling with more Harvesters soon."

Breece takes a knee, her face so bright red I can see it in even the dim lighting. "What happened back there? Were one of you able to...break through Neira's Push?"

"It was Jax, my broth—my cousin," I say. "I felt his ability."

"Family is forever." Leeyah smiles, standing taller now that she's caught her breath. "Let's get back to the camp. I'm sure the Society has enough to deal with." She rests her hand gently on my cheek. "We've had a major victory tonight."

"What about Jax?" I plead, pulling away.

"Remember that connection you felt with me? He will follow yours and find you. I have no doubt about that. Keep your awareness open. If he is in your thoughts, you can be a beacon for him."

I haven't thought of my ability like this before, but sensing others has been a part of my life since I was a little kid.

There was definitely a strong bond I felt with Leeyah. I know Jax can find me. I just hope he wants to.

***

I'm starving. Trudging through the ransacked city has left me hungry and exhausted. Breece said only a bit more, but that was close to an hour ago—I think. When it's this dark and you're running on empty, time doesn't flow the same.

"This way," Leeyah says a few steps in front of me.

I narrow my eyes. A soft blue glow halos around a door down a service alley off the main street we're on. More people wearing the dark armor plating that Leeyah and her team wears stand with their rifles pointed at us.

"Relax, guys," Leeyah says as we move closer to them. "It's us."

"What happened to your helmets and gear?" one of the men asks. "Jen and the others made it back twenty minutes ago."

"Things didn't go quite so smoothly for us," Nance says, slapping the man on his shoulder.

The guards move to the side as we approach the entrance. Leeyah turns to the other guard, asking, "Eric, did the other teams return yet?"

The man pulls off his helmet and tucks it under his arm. "Most of them have, but Lisa and Ryan's teams haven't checked in yet."

Leeyah lowers her head and pauses a moment. She sighs, then nods to Eric. "Let's get inside and rest up a bit," Leeyah says, unlatching the metal door.

The door swings in, creaking on old hinges. The blue haze emanates from several soft lanterns lining the interior corridor, doors lining each side. I follow closely behind Leeyah as Nance and Breece help Gareth. He seems a bit out of it. That long trek through the city could not have been easy with that head wound.

As we approach an opening that leads to another corridor, Nance and Breece slow.

"We'll take him to Lee in the med bay," Breece says.

Leeyah nods to Breece, then gestures for me to keep following her.

"What is this place?" I ask.

Leeyah slows and walks side by side with me. "Ironically enough, it's an old consciousness research facility. VeRx corp. Built a few of these back in the day when the Influencer ability started to show."

"Really? I've seen old billboards for VeRx in Lost Souls."

Leeyah drapes her arm over my shoulders. "I actually worked as a corporate Influencer for them."

My gaze tightens. "Why would you ever let a corporation exploit you like that?"

She stops, removing her arm. Stepping in front of me, she rests her hands on my shoulders and dips her head to get on eye level with me. "Kay, I was sixteen. I didn't know any better. The world was not like it is now. My parents thought it was a great way to do good with this strange new ability. They had no idea what to do with me. I think they were even a little afraid. Not as afraid as Laney was, though."

"So what's the deal with you and Laney?" I ask. "Why does she hate you so much?"

Leeyah sighs. Her shoulders droop, as if the weight of my question presses on her. "She always feared Push abilities. I think she resented me as well. She never liked change. I was her kid sister and she couldn't relate to me anymore. I was a freak to her."

I pause for a second and take in a deep breath. "Laney said you were a big part of how society collapsed back then. I'm sorry, I don't mean to interrogate you. I just don't understand much of what's going on in my life these days."

"Sweetie, I'm so sorry for what you've been put through." Her eyes brim with tears before she dabs them away. "My life hasn't been easy since I was young. Like you, I was thrown into some tough situations. Yes, I was in the middle of it when society collapsed, but I didn't cause it like Laney told you. Not everything from that time was bad. I met your father because of it."

My father? I haven't even thought about the fact I *have* a father in all of this. The craziness of the last few days blankets my mind.

"Is he…is he here?" I ask softly.

She releases a stuttered breath and her lips come together in a slight frown. "He died years ago. I'm so sorry. I wish you could've had a chance to meet him. He was the only thing that kept me going after I lost you. He never gave up looking for you—never."

I always wondered if I had a family. There wasn't a day that went by when I was in the orphanage system that I didn't dream about seeing them again. But finding out they existed and were actually looking for me all this time? My lips quiver as I fight back the emotion.

Leeyah wraps her arms around me. Even with her armored uniform on, her hug somehow feels right.

"We can talk more later," she says, pulling back to catch my gaze. "Let's get you some food and let you rest. I need to make sure the rest of my people are safe."

I'm not ready to stop this conversation, but I could fall over. Food and somewhere to lay my head down sound amazing, but knowing Jax is still out there will force me to keep my awareness open.

I hope he's looking for me. I need him.

The research facility has all sorts of rooms filled with equipment. One room we pass has a medical bed with restraints and all sorts of monitoring devices surrounding it. It looks like it was abandoned in a hurry. Papers linger everywhere, and most of the bedding is crumpled on the floor in piles. My mind instantly goes to the worst when it comes to any of these extinct, massive corporations. I'm sure whoever was held in that bed didn't want to be there. That's the only thing good about the world we live in now; people want to use us, but there's no need to experiment on us anymore. Influencers are well known. It's just a matter of how special you are, I guess.

Leeyah leads me to a room with empty vending machines, a small table with a few busted up chairs, and a small couch in the corner.

"I hope this is okay," she says. "This place isn't as fabulous as the Vernon Society suites, but you'll be safe here."

"It's fine. This is more what I'm used to. A couch and four walls is perfect, thank you."

Leeyah smiles and stares at me for a second. "I'm so grateful you're here. I hope we can get to know each other when this is all over."

"I'd like that."

"Well, I'm going to get out of this gear," Leeyah says, standing in the doorway. "I need to check on the others and then I'll come back with some food, alright?"

"That's great, thank you."

She walks out, and I make my way to the couch and plop down, leaning my head back. The room's quiet. I haven't felt this in a while. I'm not worried about where I am or who's after me. The only thing that prevents me from exhaling and relaxing is Jax.

I hope he's safe. I know he can handle himself, but he's been through a lot. He needs me almost more than I need him.

Twenty minutes of staring at the walls is broken when a familiar sense washes over me. It's him—Jax is near.

I jump up and head to the door. Leeyah meets me, a smile filling her face.

"He's near," she confirms. "But you know that already."

"Yes. Yes, I do." I meet her at the door and we head down the corridor toward the main exit. Leeyah's in a more casual outfit now—a fitted, black, long sleeve top with jeans. She grabs my hand and leads us down the long hall. Before we reach the door, the guards stop us.

"Ma'am," Eric says, holding his hand up to us to get us to stop. "There's a guy outside demanding to enter. I have no idea how the patrols didn't see him coming."

"It's because he didn't want you to," I say.

11

THE PROTECTORS

JAX LOOKS TIRED. A weight pulls on his eyelids and his shoulders dip down. A soft smile struggles to inch over his lips as he looks at me.

"Are you ok?" I ask

"I don't know. I've seen better days."

I put my arms around him and pull him in close to me. He returns the embrace and we stay like that for a moment, not saying a word. Releasing him, I take a step back to collect myself.

Leeyah moves to my side at the entrance. "Come in. Get warm."

"Thanks," Jax says.

Leeyah leads us down the corridor into a different converted office space. The room is set up like mine, but a bit smaller, with a low cot instead of a couch.

"I'll let you catch your breath and give you a minute," Leeyah offers. "I'll go grab some food for you both."

I smile at her as she walks out and then pivot to follow Jax to the cot at the back of the space. He sits down and leans back against the wall. I take a seat next to him, but rest my forearms on my legs as I lean over.

"You saved us," I say, looking down at my feet. "We were dead."

He sits forward, locking his arms, grabbing the edge of the cot's frame to steady his tired body. "I'm sorry I left. I never should've left you."

I straighten up and turn to him, resting my hand on top of his. "Don't say that. You've been through so much. This has to be impossible for you."

He takes a deep breath. "Doesn't matter. I should've never left you alone without knowing you were safe. Farren would've never forgiven me if you—"

"Hey, it's ok. I'm fine, and it's because of you."

Jax mentioning Farren tightens my core. A coolness fills me as my emotions stir with the thought of him. I've had so little time to think about him or Amanda over the past couple days.

"So who are these people?" he asks. "Are we safe here?"

"I trust Leeyah, but I haven't had a minute to figure things out."

Jax sits tall now, stretching his back before scooting back on the cot to lean against the wall once more.

"This isn't the family reunion we planned on, huh?" Jax asks.

I let myself lean back against the wall and rest my head on his shoulder. "Nope, not really."

A soft chuckle flickers through his fatigued body as he stares forward. We sit for a minute, zoning out as we soak up a moment of quiet.

"What are we going to do now?" he asks, looking down at me. There's an uncertainty on his face which I've not seen from him before. He's the one with the answers, not me. He needs me to be there for him, and I will.

"Let's regroup here," I suggest. "We'll figure out who these people really are and go from there. All I know right now is I miss our friends. We need to get a message out to them somehow."

Before Jax can respond, Leeyah walks in carrying a tray with two steaming bowls. A savory scent fills the small room, overloaded with fresh herbs that tickle my nose, my mouth watering.

She sits on a chair to the side of the cot and rests the tray on a makeshift end table that's no more than a dusty box. "I know this is not the five course meal that my sister probably pampered you with, but this soup is one of my favorite things to make."

Homemade food, hospitality, a warm smile— everything you want from a mother, but nothing in my life is what it seems. I can't completely let my guard down.

"That smells wonderful," Jax says, reaching out a hand. "May I?"

"Of course," Leeyah replies with a smile.

Jax grabs a bowl and hands it to me before he reaches for the other. Heat radiates off the glass, warming my hands. The amber liquid swirls as I pull it closer to me.

"Thanks," I say to Jax, then turn to Leeyah. "This smells delicious."

"Please, eat up." Leeyah gestures to our bowls.

Jax is the first to dig in. The metal spoon clanks against the edge of the bowl as he slowly stirs the soup. He tastes a spoonful and closes his eyes. "Amazing," he says before diving back in for more.

I can't wait any longer. I'm starving. I dip my spoon into the creamy liquid. When I take a sip, I completely understand what Jax feels. A buttery wash of joy coats my throat. The blend of spices excites every taste bud.

Before I realize it, the bowl's empty and I haven't said a single word since starting. I scrape at the contours of the glass, not wanting it to end. I tilt my head up and see Leeyah grinning at me, her forearms planted on her thighs. Quickly, I run the back of my hand over my mouth and pull myself upright before smiling back.

"There's more," she offers. "We can get seconds in a bit."

"Thanks, but I'm full," I lie, wanting to steal whatever's left in Jax's bowl. "It was perfect."

"Yeah, it was just what I needed," Jax adds. "Thank you."

Leeyah takes our bowls and sets them aside. She's having a hard time not staring at me, but diverts her eyes whenever I catch her at it.

"I assume you would like to know more about my group?" Leeyah asks.

"Please. We need to know what we're involved in," Jax says. "We've been thrown from one thing to the next. We'd like to get a handle on this."

I rest a hand on Jax's shoulder. "We don't want any more surprises."

Leeyah pulls her chair closer to Jax and me on the cot. "Alright then. Let me start by saying we didn't destroy the world like my sister says we did." She glances at Jax before returning her gaze to me. "The Humanity's Protectors started out as an extremist group that wanted to end the corporate control of Influencers. They did some pretty radical stuff that I was not part of. When I was a kid, I was gullible, and got caught up with this group."

She pauses for a moment, trying to gather the sudden wash of emotion that rises over her face.

"My parents were killed by the very same corporation they had let me work at as a corporate Influencer. I was lost."

She goes on to tell us how she was thrown from one mess to the next until she decided enough was enough. She got out and headed back home.

"If you left the Humanity's Protectors so long ago, why are you with them now?" I ask.

She looks up, her eyes brimming with tears. "Your father. He helped me realize something good could come from the dread that surrounded society back then."

I pull back a bit. "How did he die?" I ask plainly.

Leeyah reaches out and takes my hand, pulling it into her lap. "He died a few years ago. He never stopped believing we would find you. He never got to see his beautiful daughter all grown up."

Hot tears spill down my cheek. I quickly wipe them away with my free hand, trying to pretend they were never there. "Who was he? What was he like?"

"His name was Sam, and he was the most caring person I knew. If it wasn't for him, I would've been wasting away while the world blew up around me."

"Was he an Influencer?" Jax asks.

Leeyah narrows her gaze on Jax. "Yes. He could feel the presence of others, even if they were a great distance away. He kept us safe."

"How did he die?" I ask, quickly shifting my eyes. "You don't have to talk about it if you don't want to."

"No, it's alright. He was your father, and you deserve to know everything about him."

Jax rubs my back, completely understanding what it's like to lose family. I never knew anything about my parents—never had to lose them twice like he did. His life was shattered today, but he still shows his concern for me.

"We were trying to rescue some children from a Harvester clan," Leeyah explains. "It should've been an easy mission. Go in, disable the clan with my ability, and extract the kids. But it was a trap. A group of rogue Influencers was manipulating the clan, trying to lure in larger sector groups." She draws in a deep breath before exhaling. "When we got there, my Push couldn't counter them. We lost three people. Your father sacrificed himself so I could escape. The Influencers forced the Harvester clan to swarm him. I...I loved him so much."

Leeyah releases my hand and drops her head, trying to hide her emotions. Inching up to the edge of the bed, I place my hands on her knees. "He sounds like a great man. I'm sorry I didn't have a chance to meet him."

We sit there in silence for a minute before Leeyah straightens in her seat. She blinks away the tears and focuses on me. "I've dedicated my life to helping anyone who's been affected by the corruption and heartlessness that consumes this world, all while never giving up hope that I would find you. Now that you're back in my life, that changes everything. I don't want to fight anymore. I just want to make up for all the years we've lost."

I peek at Jax before looking back at Leeyah. "I want that too, but this isn't over yet. We have to dismantle the Vernon Society. We have to stop her. Maybe there's a glimmer of humanity left in her."

Jax purses his lips and nods. He's my family too, and just because I found my mother, it doesn't mean I have to give up on him or the friends we left behind.

"I know," she says softly. "You remind me so much of your father. The pureness in your heart is unrelenting. I saw it right away."

Jax leans forward to look at me. "Thanks, Kaylin."

I smile at him and turn back to Leeyah. "But can we dig into this tomorrow?" I ask. "Today was not fun and I am *exhausted.*"

"Of course," Leeyah says. "I'm sure we're all tired. My quarters are just down the hall. Come find me when you wake up."

She caresses the back of my hand with her thumb before standing and heading toward the door, but Jax jumps to his feet.

"Wait, do you have any working satellite phones?" he asks.

Leeyah pivots back to him, her eyes narrow. "I believe we do in the spare parts locker, but the old sat networks stopped working decades ago."

Jax takes a step closer to her. "There's an old military satellite that we've used for emergency communications. We couldn't risk using it when the Magnus Order was around. They monitored everything. But with them gone, it could work."

"What could work?" I ask.

"Farren and the others might be waiting to hear from us. If he remembered this protocol, that is."

My stomach tightens at the mention of Farren. His warm brown eyes flash through my thoughts. I shift to face Leeyah, anticipation flooding me.

"I'll go grab one," she says, turning to me with a warm smile. Somehow, she knows this is important to me. I can feel it.

After she leaves the room, I pull myself up and grab Jax's wrist, turning him to me. "Do you really think he might be listening for us?"

"For *you*, yes," he says.

I shift my eyes from him and nod, letting go of his arm. A nervous flutter replaces the pit that formed in my stomach. All I can do now is wait.

***

It feels like time has stopped and Leeyah will never return. I pace the room. Jax sits calmly on the cot. I'm about to check the hall when I feel her coming. I swallow down the anticipation simmering to the surface. She turns the corner with a scratched up, black device in her hands and a soft smile on her face.

"It has power," she says to Jax as she hands it over to him.

"Thank you," Jax mutters, examining it.

"Well, will it work?" I beg.

"There's only one way to find out."

He flips a switch on the side and taps on the dull digital display. Jax extends the phone out and slowly turns. It *beeps* and he stops. "There, we have a faint signal."

A few more taps on the device and a few seconds later, a repeating digital pulse echoes from the phone. The pulse stops and the device *clicks*. Farren's voice sounds from the speaker.

"Hello? Jax is that you? Kaylin?"

"Farren, it's us," Jax responds as he turns to me, eyes wide.

"*Jax, is it really you? Are you guys okay?*"

"Farren," I call out, walking closer to the device. "We're okay. We're okay."

"*Kaylin, what happened? Where are you?*"

"It's a long story, but we're safe now. I'm with my mother. She helped us escape from the Vernon Society."

"*Thank goodness*," Farren mutters. "*So your guys' parents weren't actually being held by the Society?*"

Jax leans in closer to the phone. "There's a lot more we have to fill you in about, but I don't know how long this phone will work. Are you guys safe down there?"

"*Caiden took care of the fallout. We got things organized before we left.*"

"Left?" Jax echoes "What do you mean?"

"*Caiden, Amanda, Ava, myself, and a few others started up north the day after you left.*" Farren says. "*We weren't going to let them take you and do nothing about it. We're about a half day from Seattle.*"

I clutch Jax's shoulder as a grin overtakes my face. They're coming. Amanda, Farren, and the others are coming! Jax turns to me, warmth flooding his face.

"You guys are really on your way up here?" I ask Farren.

"*Kay, I wasn't going to let them take you away from me. Plus, Amanda would've killed me!*"

A soft chuckle escapes from me before a rapid *beep* from the device startles me.

"Farren, our device is going to die," Jax insists. "We need to coordinate a rendezvous point."

Leeyah steps forward, grabbing our attention. "Have them meet us at the Space Needle. It's the easiest landmark for them to locate."

The device *beeps* again.

"Farren, we will meet at the Space Needle tomorrow afternoon," Jax commands. "We'll be waiting for you guys. The city is overrun by Harvesters and the Society, so stay alert."

"Okay, sounds good." Farren says. *"Stay safe."*

"Farren, please take—" I'm cut off as the device goes black.

"It's dead. I'm sorry," Jax says.

My breathing quickens. Hearing from Farren and knowing Amanda and the others are well and on their way to us is amazing, but knowing what they're walking into is terrifying.

I guess getting any sleep tonight is not happening.

12

REGROUP

THE CLOCK SAYS five am, but I'm alert and ready for the day. The air is still and frigid in my room, making getting out of bed hard, but knowing what today is about forces me up.

Leeyah left a box of clothes by the door. I didn't see her do that. I must've slept harder than I thought. Digging through the box, I find a fresh pair of dark jeans and a long-sleeved blue top that look like they should fit. The accommodations here are not quite the same as my aunt's luxury tower of control, but I don't care.

I take a deep breath, knowing this will not be fun, and tear off my outfit as fast as I can. Goosebumps instantly overtake every inch of exposed skin. Moving as quickly as my cold body can, I get dressed. It doesn't help that the new outfit is freezing cold, as it's been sitting out all night, especially the jeans. I throw on my jacket and shape my hair into a quick bun as I head out the door.

Once out in the hall, I crane my head in both directions, trying to regain my bearings. Jax's room is down to the left, and Leeyah said her room was at the end of the hall. I make my way to Jax's room and tap on the closed door.

"Just a second," Jax's muffled voice calls.

I step back just as a metal *clank* comes from his door as it swings open. Jax purses his lips and nods at me. Dark rings surround his eyes. I guess he didn't get much sleep.

"Sorry, I know it's early," I say.

"I was awake. Too much to think about."

I hug my arms around myself, trying to get warm. "Let's find Leeyah."

"Hold on," he says, looking down the hall. "Why don't we check this place out a bit first. Maybe get some breakfast."

I get it. We can't just assume everything's as safe and secure as Leeyah said it is, but being here feels different than when we were with Laney.

A rumble comes from my stomach, reminding me that despite our mission today, I still need to eat. I know that I'll need to be at full strength if I'm going to help Farren and the others at the Needle. So far the city has proven dangerous, and I can't afford to let my guard down, even with Jax by my side. A shudder steals over me.

"Yeah, let's see if we can find something to eat," I agree. Sure, Leeyah's given me fresh clothes, but so did Laney. I need to make sure that no one's planning to betray us. Even those closest to me aren't immune from having to put their own needs first.

Jax nods, smiling. "There's a door at the end of the hall that leads to the rest of the facility. We have time before we need to reach the Needle."

Despite the conflict in him, Jax exudes an air of calm as we walk down the corridor and past the room at the end that Leeyah says she's using. The door's closed, but I pause there for a moment and extend my consciousness through the immediate area, hoping to feel a sense of her warmth even if she's asleep. Only an absence meets me. Leeyah's already awake and about. There's a chance that we'll encounter her somewhere in the facility.

Jax pulls open the door and we step into a refurbished lobby that now holds several worn leather couches, leather office chairs, and vending machines that may have once been used by VeRx. Corporate Influencers may have once occupied these chairs. Perhaps Leeyah was one of them before the Protectors ripped her out of that life and threw her into war.

We pass through the empty lobby and another door, behind which there's another corridor with worn carpet and closed office doors. Paint peels off the walls, but the place gives off a cozy vibe. It's nothing like the lifeless accommodations of Laney's tower.

Two Protectors emerge from one of the offices at the end of the hall and walk past us on the way to the lobby. Black vests and helmets shield them. Guards.

Tensing, I pull to the side. One of the young men waves at us as he passes. The gesture is friendly rather than wary.

"Kaylin? Jax?" the one on the left asks.

"Yes?" I hesitantly reply. My shoulders hike as I prepare for a confrontation.

"It's okay," Jax says. "We're just checking out the place and seeing if we can find something to eat."

"The kitchen's through the door on the right," the guard says, gesturing behind him. "Leeyah told us to let you know she saved you some leftover soup."

My body remains tense even after the blond guard smiles at me and brushes past with his friend. The two of them vanish into the lobby we just left.

"Did you have anything to do with that?" I ask Jax once the two guards have gone.

"No Push involved," he says. "People sure are friendly here."

"Maybe too friendly," I say. Such warmth and caring from anyone other than my inner circle is foreign to me, like a dream that I know will be gone once I wake up and rejoin reality.

But the world may be a complicated place, and people even more so. The last forty-eight hours have been very strange, and I don't know what to believe anymore.

"Come on, Kaylin. Leeyah's already proven that she's different than Laney." Once again, conflict returns to Jax's face and posture. He looks at the wall, then at a closed door as a storm rages inside of him, peeking through the cracks it's rending in his calm mask.

Distracting him might help. "Food," I remind him. "If it's that same creamy deliciousness we had last night, well, you have to have it again." That's another strange concept that I can't wrap my mind around—regular meals. The past couple of days have changed everything.

The distraction works. Jax smiles at me. This time, I lead the way, passing another office with a cracked door. These rooms were obviously once used for VeRx's higher-ups, as some of them have long tables possibly used for meetings. A few more Protectors sit around the table, enjoying mugs of coffee. The smell wafting out is both bitter and enticing. Low chatter floats on the air and then someone laughs. Like the others, they don't mind that we're walking around the facility. For us, no doors have been locked.

The kitchen that we find behind the door to the right is medium-sized, complete with a small counter, a sink with one broken handle, and an old refrigerator covered in bright flower magnets and ceramic inspirational sayings.

"Hey, it's not bad," I say. "And the refrigerator's humming." Plenty of fridges still inhabit old buildings and houses, but most of them around Lost Souls no longer hold food unless it's non-perishable. This one still works and promises more goodies.

"Should we look around more?" Jax asks. "We need to be extra sure that we can let our guard down."

Paranoia has taken over my cousin, and now he's the one asking *me* questions. A feeling like someone's pulled the floor out from underneath me follows. "Maybe we should," I agree.

We spend a bit more time peeking into the doors of the old research area. Nobody stops us as we explore. Leeyah still doesn't show, but I sense her lingering warmth as I pace around the storage room and then a break room that's complete with a pool table and cues. Two more Protectors occupy a small table, enjoying coffee and preparing for whatever the day will bring. After that, we find a few more research rooms with the scattered papers and the tables used to hold patients in place, but they're empty, as if the Protectors don't want to linger in those areas.

Once Jax is satisfied with the safety of our current situation, we head back to the kitchen, and I find two bowls of leftover soup in the fridge. Leeyah's written my name on an index card and placed it on the first bowl, and done the same for Jax. My mood lifts as we sit at a table together and savor our food. The soup may be cold now, but the creamy taste and texture remains. Enjoying the calm before the storm, we polish off our bowls, and I tip mine to slurp the little remaining in the bottom I can't get with my spoon. My thoughts turn to Amanda, who would savor this meal just as much as I do. In Lost Souls, the two of us frequently had to skip meals.

"Kaylin," Jax asks, "how are you doing with all of this?"

That's the Jax that I know. "I don't know," I admit. "Everything's overwhelming and confusing right now. But these Protectors feel different than the Vernon Society. This place, I don't know...it just has a different kind of life to it. I guess I don't know how to react yet."

"It seems like Leeyah cares about you."

I tip the now-empty soup bowl back and forth on the table, glass tapping against the wood. A warm feeling fills my stomach and I choke up. "At least we can move freely here," I offer. "The Protectors don't seem anything like the Harvesters or Magnus or any other group I've met out there other than the rebellion." Immediately, I regret those words.

After an uncomfortable pause, Jax says, "I agree."

I breathe out, calming myself. My consciousness expands and I feel the presence of many Protectors around the facility, each one a crossroads in a web of connections. But there's something different now. The web is tense, and the sensation grows by the second. I stand and splay my fingers out on the table.

"Something's happening."

"I sense it, too," Jax says, eyeing the door.

The cafeteria door flies open, squealing on its hinges, and Leeyah bursts in, dressed in a black vest and helmet. Her mouth is bent down in a frown. Her expression alone tells me that there's a new development.

"Scouts have reported intense Harvester activity around the Space Needle," she informs us.

Leeyah doesn't need to say any more. "Our friends," I breathe.

Jax's eyes widen for a second before he regains his composure. "We're going to need your help. Please. Members of my resistance are out there. If we bring them in, they'll add value to the Protectors."

"My *friends* are out there," I add. Jax doesn't feel that Leeyah will help us on principle alone, at least not after our experience in Laney's tower.

Leeyah's warmth washes over me. There's concern and affection in the way she looks at me. "I'll assemble a couple of teams and then we'll head out. Follow me."

Jax eyes me as if he can't believe we got her to agree to this so easily. Leeyah takes us to the storage room and instructs us to put on bulletproof vests. We do. A part of me is shocked that Leeyah's even allowing me to go on this mission, but our Push abilities may be necessary to stop the Harvesters from hurting my friends.

"How many Harvesters did they report?" Jax asks.

"A few dozen," Leeyah tells him. She glances at me. There's a hardness in her eyes that's masking the warmth. "The scouts informed me there may be two or three clans heading toward the Needle from different directions. It's clear that the Harvesters have detected valuable people in the area."

The hideout's buzzing with activity as Leeyah, Jax, and I make our way to the door. Leeyah is efficient; two teams have already assembled in the corridor. Nance leads the first, a team of six, while Breece is leading the second. The teams of black-clad Protectors form two lines, ready for action. No one is questioning the *whys* of this mission.

"Ready for the fun?" Breece asks me as we head out.

"Always," I say. "What fun?"

"Well, life is ten percent what happens and ninety percent how you react to it," she quips. "That's what my father always told me."

The sun has risen enough to cast gray light on the city of Seattle. Fog embraces the surroundings, and a light drizzle that makes it difficult to see very far ahead mists the air as Leeyah and our teams exit the facility. This is a world of gray, and if we don't hurry, Farren and Amanda and the others may die in it or end up captured by Harvesters.

"Kaylin, Jax," Leeyah says, getting out attention, "we're going to need the two of you to monitor the situation. The fog might lift soon, but until then, we'll need you."

"Understood," Jax says.

Leeyah's brought us on this mission out of necessity, I'm sure of it. She doesn't want to put me in danger— that's how Sam died.

The drizzle turns to a light rain as we round a corner. I blink and see Farren behind my eyelids, making my heart swell. I'll need to do this for him.

Breathing out, I calm my emotions and force myself to focus instead on my surroundings. My consciousness expands. The task is harder with my eyes open versus closed, but with each breath, I manage to pulse my awareness outward. The presence of small animals—

possibly rats and birds and even a few cats—reveal themselves to me as points of purity and light. So far, I detect no other humans in the area other than our team. Next to me, Jax remains quiet, focusing as well.

We won't have Stratton or Neira to deal with at the Needle, right? That's my biggest hope. Even mobilizing the local wildlife won't help against the two of them.

My awareness slips every time we turn a new corner or Leeyah orders her team to fan out at the mouth of each new street. The mist seeps into my skin and hair and I'm glad for the long-sleeved shirt. Once we get going down each new street, I'm able to expand my consciousness again, enfolding the surrounding area.

As we walk, the light grows and the fog begins to lift like an ethereal curtain, revealing more of Seattle.

"Do you sense anything?" Leeyah asks me and Jax for the first time in minutes.

"Not yet," I say. "No—wait."

A small sea of human consciousness enters my web. A sense of desperation blankets me, along with an array of other emotions—anger, fear, pain.

"The Harvesters," Jax says.

"We're close to the Needle," Leeyah says. "Breece, Nance, move onto the adjacent streets and cover us."

I know why she's giving these orders. A repeat of yesterday's events would be a disaster. Blinking, I peer through the fog, now able to make out some taller buildings. A skinny tower stands behind one of the tan structures, and it takes me a moment to realize that it's a large metal disc atop three poles. The Space Needle. Our rendezvous point.

Drawing a sharp breath, I listen as footfalls fan out behind us and guns cock. Our teams are splitting, making sure no Harvesters sneak up on us. Leeyah fixes me with her gaze. "I'm detecting a large number of Harvesters."

"Me too," I say. "We have to get closer to affect them." Leeyah's abilities may still be active, but at her age, they may be fading.

"Agreed," Jax says.

Peeking around buildings on either side of us, Leeyah gives our teams hand movements to indicate that it's time to move forward. My heart races with emotion and an intense need to know what's happening to my friends. The buildings prevent me from seeing the area around the Needle, so Leeyah guides us to a large building and up a stairwell leading up the outside of it. A balcony will allow us to get a better vantage point.

As I climb the rusted metal steps, I force myself to breathe at a regular pace and expand my consciousness once again. It envelops the emotional sea of people around the Needle, and my mind wakes to a greater reality. In the confusion, I struggle to find someone who can help me observe. Many of the minds in this sea are consumed by the most basic needs—food, shelter, water. The Harvesters' awareness doesn't expand much beyond that.

At last, I detect a mind that feels more alert than the others—that of an older man who might be a clan leader.

Closing my eyes, I focus. Flashes of the Needle and then a low building fill my vision as I climb.

The stairs flatten under me. We've reached a balcony. Opening my eyes, I realize we're not far above the ground, but we're high enough to see the crowd of ragged people around the base of the Space Needle. Three different groups have converged on the weed-choked plaza. Leeyah leans over the railing of the balcony, watching, but none of them have detected us. One group wears yellow bandannas, and another has tied blue cloths around their waists to show membership in their clan. The third group wears no special colors. The size of the crowd tells me Farren and the others have attracted far too much attention while travelling through the city. All of them push around the Space Needle. The crowd shifts towards a building opposite us, a low warehouse.

"Where are they?" Jax asks. His paranoia and uncertainty has returned.

"Let me focus," I say, closing my eyes again. Even from up here, I can't see the entire plaza. Exhaling, I shove my awareness outward, encasing the madness below. The storm of emotion spreads out, and I take precious seconds to zero in on the lead man. Flashes of what he's seeing fill my mind.

A warehouse covered in graffiti spreads out before him, and Farren keeps his hands on one door. Caiden has the other, pistol drawn while Amanda stands directly behind him along with Ava and Envee. Other Resistance fighters wait, shouting at each other. Farren grimaces, struggling to hide his terror as he realizes he's going to die.

13

TORN

HEAVY GUNFIRE RIPS away my focus. My Push ends. I open my eyes, my connection to the Harvester leader broken. I can't miss the smoke rising around where the Harvesters are gathering in front of the building. Many of them have guns. The attack on my friends feels organized and over the top. More Harvesters emerge from between buildings and join the crowd. My friends are rapidly getting overwhelmed.

I look to Leeyah. She makes hand movements to the next building over, where Breece's team is emerging onto the rooftop. Then she does the same with the building to our left, where Nance's team has taken up position on an upper balcony.

"Kaylin, Jax, you need to do what you can to stop the Harvesters from reaching whoever's down there. I've signaled the others to give us rooftop support."

"Farren," I breathe, chest filling with emotion. It's possible that Leeyah hasn't seen what I have yet.

Jax shifts from foot to foot. "I'll extend my reach to keep more Harvesters from getting into the area. Kaylin, see if you can get the birds to distract the ones who are already here."

Gripping the railing, I close my eyes and focus, extending my consciousness into the sky. More gunfire *pops*, threatening to pull me out of my state, but I breathe harder, focusing on the sound of the wind with all my being.

At last, the commotion fades as I rise into the sky, searching outward until my awareness touches dozens— no, hundreds—of pure points of light; a large flock of birds. I merge with them, and then I'm sailing through the mist and the rising fog. Bits of blue sky shine through before the birds plunge through a low cloud and emerge again, facing the plaza with the Space Needle.

The Harvesters appear as ants swarming around the warehouse, their weapons held aloft like tiny pieces of food they're bring back to their nest. Smokes rolls across the plaza, and sparks of light flash from and then fade into the dark space between the cracked open doors. My friends are fighting back.

I order my bird soldiers into the fray, their songs turning to war cries as they dive into the throng. Pecking and clawing at any exposed skin they can find, the birds force the Harvesters away from the warehouse doors.

The Harvesters are screaming, flailing their arms, crashing into each other and trampling those who fall. The Resistance fights and the Protectors continue spraying bullets into the crowd. The Harvesters are slipping in their own blood, tripping over their own comrades.

And then true chaos breaks out.

A Harvester woman in a yellow bandanna strikes another member of her clan over the head with the butt of her gun. Her face contorts in a terrified grimace. More Harvesters fall to the ground, dropping their weapons and curling into balls of fear. Whimpering fills the spaces between gunshots and bird cries. One man throws another to the ground and strikes him repeatedly with his fists before screaming and running from the Plaza.

Ava. She must be here, using her Push to disperse the crowd. She's the only one I know who can fill crowds with pure terror like this.

The remaining Harvesters continue to scream and swat at the birds as if they're tiny dragons swooping from the sky. I can only imagine what our combined Pushes are making them see and feel. The crowd thins. Gunshots continue to sound from the warehouse and the balconies, dropping a few more Harvesters to the concrete, but within moments, they've all gone.

Silence settles in. Blackbirds begin landing between the weeds and hopping over to investigate some of the bodies. Gross. I retract my Push and find myself standing on the balcony again, eyes closed. I continue to grip the rusty railing.

"Kaylin, you can use your Push on animals?" Pride fills Leeyah's voice and urges me to open my eyes. I face her to find she's smiling. "Well done. You and Jax stopped that Harvester attack within two minutes. Even in my younger years, I couldn't have managed such a feat."

I almost ask her what exactly her Push can do, but there's a more pressing matter, and it's Farren and Amanda and the others. "Some of that was Ava," I say.

"Ava?" she echoes questioningly.

Jax remains silent as he paces up and down the balcony. I know he's focusing on keeping new Harvesters out of the area, but I doubt that after Ava's push any of them will *want* to return.

"You'll meet her," I say. "Come on. We have to get down there before they decide to leave." They won't, now that I think about it. The invading birds alone will tell Farren and Amanda that I'm here, but I want to see for sure that they're safe and unharmed.

My heart races as I anticipate jumping into Farren's arms, but it's worry that propels me down the metal steps. Once on the pavement, I race for the warehouse, hands up. I run because of Farren and Amanda, but I also run because of the bodies and the blood. Maybe I didn't kill anyone this time, but I helped to make this happen. My distraction got many of these Harvesters killed.

Birds scatter into flight at the sound of my steps. I don't have to be in their minds to know they'll return later for a sample of blood and flesh.

I stop when a gun points out of the warehouse doors. Jax appears beside me, and then shoves me back, blocking the path of the gun.

"It's us!" I shout. "It's okay! These people with us are the Protectors. They freed us from the Vernon Society."

"There's no need to shoot," Jax adds. "I'm still the leader of this Resistance." He speaks with the calm confidence I'm used to.

The gun in the doorway lowers and then the metal door slides open. Farren stands in a rectangle of darkness, gun lowered and blinking in the light.

"Kaylin?"

I run to him, heart swelling. He spreads his arms to catch me as I dive into his embrace. He traveled all this way and risked his life to get to me.

"Kaylin!" he gasps, wrapping his hands around the small of my back. He's got a slight sunburn, but the warmth remains in his brown eyes. "Can I have this pleasure?"

"Shut up," I say with a smile.

He closes his eyes and lowers his face to mine. I purse my lips as we kiss, and my heart beats against Farren's powerful chest as he pulls me into the darkness of the warehouse, away from prying eyes. Farren tastes like ancient forest, like the realm of the Resistance, like the place where I learned to find a new family for the first time.

We come up for air. Even though it's dark in here, I can still see Farren's mouth turn up into a smile. "I missed you. That made that kiss so much better." Releasing me, he turns to the others in the doorway. "Who are your new friends?"

Someone shuffles nearby. "I'm sorry, but there aren't any hotel rooms here, you two."

A silhouette stands next to us and I don't have to see him to know he's grinning. "Hey, Caiden." I'm glad that he's teasing. It means that no one I know likely died, and I know it was probably him who ordered everyone to retreat into the warehouse. That probably saved their lives.

"Well, since Jax abandoned us, I had to take the lead," he says. "Do you think I should get a promotion? I'm sure the leader's sister could put in a good word."

"Not yet," Jax says. "Maybe later, I'll think about it." He moves to stand right behind Caiden in a mock threatening manner.

"Oh, and there's something else, too," Caiden adds. "Owen has a new toy for us to try out. I'll have to tell you about it later."

"A new toy?" I ask.

"The man's a genius," Farren tells me.

Outside, the Protectors draw closer. Boots tap the concrete and someone makes a comment about all the birds. All of us will have a lot of explaining to do to each other. Farren wraps an arm around my waist and pulls me close.

"Hold it," Amanda says, charging out of the darkness. "You can't hog Kaylin after all this time. Release her, now."

Farren obeys and puts both hands up. Amanda's carrying a gun, but she sets it down on the dirty floor of the warehouse as she glares at me and waits. The two of us hug and Amanda tries to lift me and spin me in a circle.

"That's not going to work," I say.

"You're still a kid to me," she says. "I was so worried about you after you got into the FlexViper."

Amanda pulls me back into her and squeezes me harder than she has ever before. She releases me, as she wipes a tear from her cheek.

"I'm ok." I smile at her. "I'm sorry I left you like that."

It's something I don't want to imagine. Guilt still fills me over leaving Amanda behind, but it wasn't as if I'd a choice to go with Miya and Stratton. It must have killed her inside to know the girl she's protected since fleeing the orphanage went straight to her worst nightmare.

"Well, we're here now," I say. "We never meant to stay with the Vernon Society. They aren't any better than the Magnus Order."

"Did...did you meet your parents?" Amanda asks, releasing me enough to let me breathe more easily.

"It's...complicated," I say. "Jax and I have a lot of explaining to do."

Amanda grins. "Jax isn't going to take my place as favorite sibling, is he?"

"He's my cousin, actually. Not my brother."

"*What?*"

"I told you we have a lot of explaining to do."

A dark-skinned figure with striking white tattoos walks past. Ava. There's one more major thing I have to do before getting to the explaining part. As someone who had to witness Maddux's death, I feel it's my job to comfort her. Taking a breath, I hold up a finger to Amanda to let her know it's going to be a minute or two.

Ava walks over to an old crate and sits. She's different from when I saw her last. Instead of walking with purpose, she moves like someone who's been hollowed out. She must not have had much time to come to grips with the situation before everyone decided to come after me and Jax. I imagine that if I lost Farren or Amanda, I'd turn into a shell of myself, too.

"Ava," I say. A lump forms in my throat as the horrible image of Maddux's body fills my mind. "I'm sorry about Maddux."

Ava nods. "Thanks." There's not much life in her eyes, and I'm amazed she could still deliver an effective Push against the Harvesters. Then again, her ability *is* fear. Grief might have even amplified her power in a way.

The feeling that I haven't said and done enough sweeps over me. "If there's anything I can do—"

Ava stands abruptly, swallowing hard. "We don't have time to let our fear consume us. That's what happened to the Harvesters out there. We Influencers need to focus on making this world a better place rather than on our own sadness and fear, so that there are no more senseless deaths like Maddux's."

I can tell Ava's doing her best to hold it together. Before, her words were filled with passion and made me feel better about my Influencer abilities. Now she's reciting lines and going through the motions.

She turns her attention to the Protectors, who are walking through the warehouse doors with caution. Leeyah leads, and I have to turn away from Ava to clear things up.

"Guys, this is Leeyah," I announce. I'm proud to introduce her. Leeyah's already proven herself many times over. "She's with the Protectors, and she's the one who got us out of the Vernon Society."

Leeyah smiles. Jax rushes over to stand beside her, sending a calming smile at the few Resistance fighters standing in a ring inside the door. I'm glad he's here to defuse the tension.

"This is my Aunt Leeyah," he says.

"What?" Amanda asks in shock. "Are you saying that *Leeyah* is Kaylin's mother? I have competition after all?"

"It's *complicated*," I repeat.

"Once we all get to a safe place, then we'll discuss," Leeyah says. "Jax, are you holding the Harvesters back? Do you feel any of them returning?"

Her words bring me back into the seriousness of the moment. We're still in a large city, one of the most dangerous areas for anyone to travel through. A dark cloud seems to fall over the room, dampening the mood, and as we stand there in silence, it only deepens.

"No, I don't feel them returning," Jax says. His expression changes. "But I do—"

"What's the point of getting back to safety?" one of the Resistance fighters interrupts. "This is a hopeless world. Soon enough, we're all going to die and watch everyone we love die." The young man faces Ava. "You already know that. Once you lose someone, you see reality for what it really is."

Ava puts her hands up. "Stanley, you need to calm down." She looks to Jax for help, but Stanley draws his weapon.

"Why bother?" he asks. "That's all this world is. Loss and heartbreak. The times worth living in are over. This world belongs to the corrupt now. The rest of us have a bleak existence of hiding and surviving like rats. It's time to free all of us from this nightmare."

The sense of dread in the room deepens. I feel as if black pulses are trying to race through my being. Stanley turns his weapon on one of the other Resistance fighters. A look of pure agony comes over the young man's face as his finger curls around the trigger. Jax rushes over, trying to stop it, but it's too late.

Stanley fires.

The other Resistance fighter—a man in his thirties—jolts and falls, grasping his chest. Stanley has delivered a fatal shot.

"It's Stratton!" I shout. He's nearby and using his Push on the non-Influencers and non-implanted of the group. The dread grows as many of the Protectors shift around in the darkness as if trying to escape. Breece grabs at the doorway and leans against it, tears streaming down her cheeks. Envee, the blond girl, looks to Breece and back to me. It's as if she's begging me to stop this. Amanda lets out a sob and falls into Ava's embrace.

I close my eyes and breathe out. As I do, my consciousness expands through the warehouse and the immediate area, enfolding everyone within it. The Resistance fighters and the Protectors are more aware than the Harvesters, making them easier to target. I beam thoughts of happiness and hope into them. The mood lightens and the air grows less heavy as I counteract Stratton's Push. The sense of black dread vanishes and Amanda sighs in relief, bringing me back into the moment.

Upon opening my eyes, I find that Leeyah's looking at everyone in turn. I take a breath of the lighter air, waiting for Jax and Leeyah to figure out what to do.

"They know we're here," I say. "The Harvesters must have told the Vernon Society what's going on." It was that, or the activity alerted Stratton and perhaps Neira. "If Stratton's nearby, then Neira won't be far behind."

Leeyah appears to think for a moment. She paces back and forth a couple of times as she frowns. "We need to fall back before Neira can stop our Pushes," she reasons. "We can't afford to lose any more fighters."

"What have I done?" Stanley asks, throwing down his gun. He backs away. "I killed Norman!"

"It wasn't you. It was Stratton," Jax tells him, taking his arms and standing on the weapon. "Leeyah's right. We need to leave the area, but we don't know which direction Stratton and Neira are in."

Stanley can barely stand. His knees threaten to give out. "I killed Norman!"

"Keep it together," Jax says. "We need to move. Someone take his gun."

"We need a distraction," Leeyah says. "Jax, you need to allow the Harvesters back into the area. I think they were acting on their own and not with Stratton. Do we have any other Influencers here?"

"Me," Envee says, raising her hand before Ava can speak. "I can amplify."

"Then do so," Leeyah instructs. "We're going to need a large distraction if we're going to get out of here undetected. Kaylin, you need to draw their attention back to this area as well."

The idea sounds horrible and it's a tough call, but I find that I'm trusting Leeyah. She's gotten us this far, and Harvesters are better than Stratton and Neira.

Envee peels herself from the wall, waving me and Jax toward the door. "Come on!" The three of us glance at each other as we gather in the doorway. Time's running out, so we have to move quickly.

I close my eyes and allow my awareness to once again expand. I sense the warmth and caring from Leeyah, and it's hard to move my consciousness out to the surrounding area. There's no one else in the plaza other than some lingering birds. Stratton's Push hangs at the periphery like living, inky darkness, waiting for Neira to disable us so it can do its worst. I still can't sense them, but then a wave of consciousness sweeps me outward. Envee's Push.

My awareness grows into an ocean as she helps. Now I sense them. Harvesters—hundreds or maybe more—jostle each other, desperate to escape the terror in the plaza. I focus on thoughts of desperation and desire, things that the Harvesters can understand. What they need can be found in the plaza, and the Space Needle becomes a beacon of hope. Jax and I blanket the crowd with these thoughts, and Envee's amplification tucks them in.

The human mass shifts toward us.

"Kaylin!"

Amanda jars me out of my Push as she tugs on my arm. Leeyah and the non-implanted fighters stand behind her in the semi-dark, desperate to leave.

"There's movement out there," Caiden says, looking out the open door. "I think we have the distraction that we need."

Jax shakes his head, pulling out of his Push.

"Go, go, go!" Envee shouts.

We follow Caiden and Leeyah out the door and into the open. Pale light falls over us as the fog continues to lift, taking away our cover. Farren appears beside me and slips his hand into mine as we run toward the Needle. A low rumble fills the air, and I nearly trip over a Harvester body.

"Is that footsteps?" Farren asks me.

I gulp. "Yes."

Movement flashes in every corner of my vision as Harvesters fill the alleys and begin to pour into the plaza from every opening. The rumbling sound intensifies. I tighten my grip on Farren's hand as the city bleeds desperate human life into its center.

14

COLLIDE

OUR FREE SPACE is rapidly running out. There's no telling how Jax has made all these Harvesters feel, but it's clear from their faces that they believe their salvation is somewhere in the plaza. Envee's ability to amplify mine has had a greater effect than I expected.

Several rough-looking men step over the bodies as if they're just pieces of garbage or concrete. One of them holds a rusty crowbar. Another walks with a shotgun banging against his ripped jeans. Chunks of rebar and concrete, glass bottles, and wooden boards make up the weapons of choice for dozens of others.

We back against the base of the Needle. Coldness seeps through my shirt and promises death.

"Oops," Envee says.

Leeyah faces me. "Distract them and create an opening. I trust you, Kaylin."

The horde shuffles closer. I press against Farren, who wraps his fingers around my arm. Our ring of safety shrinks with each second. Jax nods at me, giving me silent encouragement. Ava trains her attention on the Harvesters to our left, and many of them double back, clawing at the air and screaming at invisible monsters. The noise mixes with the shuffling of feet and the tapping of two-by-fours.

Breathing out, I face the alley between a couple of tall apartment buildings. There's an opening there without any Harvesters pouring through it. That vein has already emptied its blood into the plaza. Seconds tick down as I close my eyes and focus. The screams of the terrified continue. None of the Harvesters speak. Our collective Push has been more effective than any I've seen.

"Hurry, Kaylin," Leeyah urges.

My awareness expands into the throng like water wrapping around stones in a river. Envee gives me no input, but I only need to clear a path to the alley. The distraction has to be maintained to keep Stratton off us. The cries of those under Ava's Push fade as my focus improves. I tell them this path offers no hope and everyone needs to move to the side. The dulled awareness of the Harvesters shifts, opening a route to the alleyway.

"Come on!" Farren shouts, pulling on my arm.

My eyes flutter open and he's tugging me toward the new opening in the crowd. The screams return as I rejoin this reality and run along with Farren, Amanda, and Breece past a couple of bodies. Pumping my legs, I try to look back to see who's following. We're headed in the opposite direction from the screaming, away from the effect of Ava's Push. Breece holds her weapon in front of her, but there's no need. The Harvesters, weapons in hand, step aside for us, their eyes remaining dulled and focused on other Harvesters. Nobody knows what to do or where to go. Confusion reigns.

The mouth of the alley is choked with weeds and sun-faded, torn garbage bags. We bolt into the shelter as Farren maintains his protective grip on my arm, but none of the Harvesters come after us. Concern sweeps over me as I turn my head to see who's come with us. Stanley and two of the Protectors have joined us, but no one else has made it.

The screams continue in the plaza. Harvesters on the opposite side of the Needle scatter and leave an opening, but before I can see whether Leeyah and the others are taking it, the Harvesters who opened up for us close the escape route. Two women focus on us first. One of the them tugs on the sleeve of a large, burly man holding a shovel.

"Don't stop!" Breece orders, kicking a trash bag out of the way. "I'm not going to have anyone die on my watch." She waves us down the alley, where it ends in a T-junction.

"But Leeyah!" I shout. "Jax! Envee!"

"Kay, if we don't move, then none of us will see the others again," Amanda says, grabbing my other arm as we continue to jog away from the fray.

Seven of us flee through the alley. I'm not sure how long my Push will last, but it's clear that more and more of the Harvesters are focusing on us now. Breece pauses at the junction and looks both ways, then waves us to the right and shoots us a smile. "Clear." Her perky attitude's doing wonders to calm my nerves.

Amanda releases my arm, but Farren keeps his hand on mine. "I'm sure Leeyah and Jax will be fine," he says as we slow. So far, it doesn't seem that the Harvesters have entered the alley behind us—yet. The buildings tower over us and make me feel as if I'm navigating the world's most dangerous maze. This is a city, the very place Amanda and I have spent our lives avoiding.

After turning a few more corners, we slow. The thunder of the Harvesters' feet fades behind us. Farren slips his hand into mine and squeezes. "So..." he starts with an infectious smile. He nods to Breece. "You have good taste in friends."

My mind keeps going to Jax and Leeyah. Farren's doing his best to make sure I don't panic and run back to them. He knows how I am, and I get that he's trying to distract me. I appreciate him for that.

"Breece," I tell him. "She's with the Protectors. She helped Leeyah—she helped my mother rescue me from the Vernon Society."

"Are you talking about me?" Breece asks from ahead. "I don't like it when people do that." Even though I can't see her face, I can tell she's smiling. "Do I have to separate you two?"

"We sure are," Farren says. "And no. You're not going to do that."

It amazes me that Breece manages to maintain such a good attitude in such a brutal world. She's the opposite of Stratton. Even though she's not an Influencer, it's impossible not to feel better around her.

But focus is needed here.

"Look," I say. "It's too quiet around here. I don't like that."

"That's because you and Jax and Envee moved all the Harvesters out of this area," Farren tells me. "It worked. We distracted whoever it was that you needed to distract."

I realize that I haven't told him about Neira yet. Farren knows all about Stratton from Talas, though.

"Keep sensing out the area, Kaylin," Breece instructs. "We need you right now. This is that ninety percent of life that I mentioned."

How we react.

Her words sink in. I'm the only Influencer in our party. We go silent as Breece and the other two Protectors move ahead of us, guns raised as they peek around alley corners and narrow side streets. Since it's impossible to close my eyes and navigate this mess at the same time, I have to try to focus on our surroundings as I breathe regularly and step over more debris. My awareness expands a few streets around us. I feel a few people in the buildings. They have a brighter awareness than the Harvesters and feel similar to the animals I've sensed in the area. Children, most likely. None of them show themselves to us. I've gotten the sense that the kids of the city spend most of their time hiding from rival Harvesters rather than playing.

Breece waves us around another corner. "If we're going to meet up with Leeyah and Nance's teams again, it will be at the research facility," she says. "I'm confident that with so many Influencers in one group, they were able to escape the Harvesters." Breece winks at me. "I'm sure you'll see Leeyah and Jax again. I like those two."

"You and Jax would get along," I tell her.

Speaking makes me lose focus, but I'm glad she's reassuring me. So far, I'm more than just a weapon to the Protectors and to Leeyah. They're so different from the Vernon Society and Laney.

We're walking down a narrow side street lined with abandoned shops when the dread hits me like a wall of invisible darkness. I stop in the street. Breece and the two Protectors continue walking for a moment before they also stop. Farren eyes me, as does Amanda.

"It's him," I say.

"Stratton? That rat?" Amanda asks. She turns her head to check the surrounding stores, many of which have broken windows, but not before I catch the terror dilating her pupils.

Breece raises her weapon and backs away, trying to escape the cloud of terror and despair. "It's *him,*" she hisses, teeth clenching. Her positive attitude is gone.

But it's too late to escape. The dusty door to an abandoned ice cream parlor swings open and Stratton steps out. He wears the black jacket of the Vernon Society, black hair slicked back above the intense gaze he trains on me. The very air thickens in his presence.

Stanley drops his weapon and sinks to his knees. The other fighter, a young woman in her twenties, trembles as she tries to fight the effect of his Push. Amanda bites her lip and backs away.

"Farren," I say, "take her weapon."

He lets go of my hand as Stratton nods at me. "Kaylin," he greets me. "I was hoping we'd meet again under better circumstances."

"I want nothing to do with you," I say, trying to hold his attention as Farren, unaffected by Stratton's Push thanks to his block implant, wrestles the gun from Amanda's grasp. It's up to me and him to stop our fighters from killing themselves and each other. I think of Ava's emptiness and wonder if that's what I'll be like if I lose Farren or Amanda. The thought pumps terror through me.

"None of you know a thing about me," Stratton snaps. Hatred fills his eyes as he paces. "Why are you so quick to judge?"

Another door opens behind us. Weapons cock. Whirling, I find five Vernon Society guards in their black jackets and beanies pointing their guns at us. We're surrounded, and under the throes of Stratton's Push, Breece, Stanley, and the other fighter are helpless to fight back. The same goes for Amanda, who leans against the brick building with silent tears running down her cheeks.

"We're done," Stanley says.

"This is hopeless," Breece adds. "He's already killed—"

"Leave them alone!" I shout. "If it's me that you want—"

"Kaylin!" Farren shouts, interrupting me.

An overwhelming presence fills my awareness. The faint thunder of feet grows louder. Rats scatter and run past us, trying to find shelter. Stratton looks right and left, trying to determine the source of the sound, but I know what's happening. Farren and I share a glance.

The Harvesters have left the plaza. They're coming after those who have worked their Influencer powers on them. The two who saw our group leaving must have mustered the others, and now they don't just want what we have, they want revenge. The anger pulsing through the air is undeniable.

"Sir," one of the Vernon guards says, "incoming threat."

I press against Farren. Amanda sniffles and peels herself from the wall as the heaviness in the air defuses. Stratton's losing focus on his Push. One of the Harvesters must have heard me yelling at Stratton, or they had their children track us from the rooftops. I'll never know the answer, but if we're going to live without Envee here to amplify my Push, we need to do the unthinkable.

"Harvesters incoming from the north," a tall Vernon guard says.

"And the east," another adds in panic.

"There's a possible escape route ahead of us," Stratton says, whirling. Now that the Harvesters are coming, I'm no longer a big concern.

But a human flow emerges from between the buildings ahead. The Harvesters must have surrounded us the moment we stopped moving. Breece picks up her weapon again. The burly man leads the pack, holding a board with nails sticking out of it. Pure hatred contorts his features into something that will forever haunt my nightmares.

There are too many of them. I'll never do a successful Push on my own.

"Stratton, we need your help," I grit out.

He looks back and forth, turning in a circle as fear washes over his face.

"You need to keep the Harvesters back or we're all going to die," Farren insists, handing back Amanda's gun. Then he faces the Vernon guards. "You, too, Kaylin. Do what you can."

Footfalls fill the street behind us. The thought of working with Stratton fills me with nausea, but if there's anything I've learned in the past few weeks, it's that doing the worst is sometimes necessary in order to survive. These Harvesters won't merely rob us, they want to see us burn and suffer. The leader has made that clear already with that nail-studded board. If Ava were here, she'd tell me the same thing.

"Kaylin, hurry," Amanda urges.

"I'll help," Stratton says. He looks at his guards and nods. "Open fire!"

Gunshots pop. The pavement sparks as the Vernon guards fire on the crowd. Our fighters don't yet use their weapons, but Stratton has no problem with killing, even if it's unnecessary.

Screams rise from the Harvesters. Some of them are just people caught up with the wrong crowd; I'm sure of that. But I close my eyes, exhaling, as I slip my hand into Farren's. Even he fades away as I expand, sweeping over and around the panicked, angry Harvesters. Many of them charge. Others flee from the gunfire. The Vernon Society won't hold them off for long.

"Stay back to back!" Breece shouts.

I'm glad I'm facing away from Stratton, that I can't see what he's doing. Focusing, I let out a breath and take my thoughts from him. I continue sending thoughts to the Harvesters. They don't need to hurt us to move on with their lives. I enfold the presences of the people closest to us and project thoughts and feelings of forgiveness to them. I'm sorry that I've manipulated them. Many slow and pause, but it's not fast enough. I search for the aware leader in the crowd, but he's not on my side.

I do detect a couple of women more attuned to this vast reality than the others. My awareness goes to them, and my Push intensifies as I hook into the living web. Forgiveness is the only way these Harvesters are going to survive. Many of them turn back and flee into the city's cracks, returning to their safe hiding places. The crowd thins. The gunshots from the Society are faint, and they keep firing even as the Harvesters turn and clear the street behind us. Most go out of my range, but a few take cover in alleys with nothing other than a desire to survive the situation.

Opening my eyes, I see the empty street. The Vernon guards keep their rifles raised, ready to open fire again. Smoke fills the air. Two bodies lie on the cobbled surface and a trail of blood leads into an alley. My heart aches as I think of the person who hobbled away with an injury they may not have the resources to heal.

Cries of despair follow. It takes everything I have to face Stratton's side of the fight. Harvesters battle one another on his side, hitting each other with boards and other blunt objects. The burly man strikes another guy with the board repeatedly, screaming about freeing him from this bleak existence. One of the Harvester women turns her pistol on herself. Still others run away, crying and screaming, as Stratton fixes his soulless glare on our common enemies.

"Don't look," Farren says, pulling me close. My eyes meet his flannel shirt and I bury myself against his chest, trying to shut out the horrible noises. The air is so thick that I can barely breathe. Farren combs the ends of my hair with his fingers, but he's shaking. We're disgusted and terrified together. He yells something at Breece and Stanley, but over the noise, I can't make it out. Footfalls rush past me and more hitting noises follow. A gunshot goes off very close, but Farren won't allow me to look.

He holds me close to him so that he takes up my entire world.

At last, after an eternity in some horrible underworld, the cries of despair and anger die down. Farren's grip loosens and silence falls. For the first time in what feels like hours, I can lift my head.

Bodies litter Stratton's side of the fight. Blood paints the concrete. Makeshift weapons lie in front of stores where people once window shopped and got together with friends. There's no counting the ones that didn't flee. Trying might drive me to insanity.

"Remain where you are," Breece orders.

Turning my head away from the carnage, I realize that Breece, Amanda, Stanley, and the other fighter have wrestled the Vernon Society guards' weapons away from them while they weren't paying attention to us. All five of the guards flee down the street as Amanda fires, but misses. She growls with rage and fires again. The bullet shatters one of the few unbroken windows on the street instead of finding its mark.

Stratton takes a step forward and I face him again. "So much for working together, huh?" he asks, amused.

Farren charges the Vernon Influencer, hitting him over the head with the butt of the weapon with a hollow-sounding *thunk*.

Stratton staggers back, eyes rolling up into his head. He crumples to the cobble, landing in a heap.

Farren doesn't pause to admire what he's done. "Come on," he says. "Grab him, and let's get out of here before he wakes up or the Society comes back with reinforcements."

15

UNDERSTANDING

STRATTON REMAINS UNCONSCIOUS as Stanley and Farren each grab him under the arm and drag him through the remains of the city. His boots scrape on the cobble as we vacate the area. Stratton groans once and Stanley flinches, but the young Resistance fighter doesn't let go. There's a haunted look on his weathered face, and it's clear that he has revenge on his mind. I don't need to expand my consciousness to know that.

Farren glances at me as we cut down another alley and toward some stairs that lead into the darkness underneath the city, a dank, musty smell emerging from it. I know why he's letting Stanley help handle Stratton. He doesn't want me to have to get anywhere near such a monster.

"The subway," Breece tells me. "Even the Harvesters don't often go there. It's too infested with rats and there's nothing of value. Not to mention they flood easily." She glares at Stratton. Her attitude's shifted since he showed.

"Stratton can join them," I say, watching as Amanda wrinkles her nose. "He's a rat." Hope fills me that perhaps he can still hear.

"Wait, what are you planning?" Breece asks. "Some good old-fashioned interrogation?"

"Perhaps," Farren replies.

"Don't you think that's dangerous?" Breece continues. "Right now we have only one Influencer with us, and I don't want her to have to handle him alone."

"I agree," Farren says, sharing a glance with Amanda. It's as if the three of them are having a vote about not making me handle this.

A protest starts on my lips, but then I realize that I don't want to deal with Stratton alone either. The thought of three people looking out for me boggles my mind. "Having more than one Influencer keeping him under control would make sense."

Breece and Amanda both smile at me. "Good thinking, squirt," Amanda says.

"Hey!"

"I'm going to be a little while, then," Breece says. "I need someone to help me gather the others." She waves the other female fighter along with her and vanishes into a nearby alley. In a way, I'm glad she's gone. If Stratton wakes, that's one less person he can drive to do unthinkable things.

As we wait, Farren and Stanley continue to check on Stratton, taking his pulse and pushing his eyelids back. Our group waits at the entrance to the subway tunnels.

"I hope she knows where the others might have gone," I say.

"I'm sure these Protectors have multiple meeting points," Amanda reassures me. "The others would have gone to the nearest one they could. It might take Breece a while to round them all up."

But it doesn't. It turns out that Leeyah, Jax, and the others have stayed together since the separation. Breece got instructions before the mission to find them at a certain warehouse in that event. The Protectors are planners, and that makes me breathe a big sigh of relief when she, Nance, Caiden, and everyone else pour into the alley.

Leeyah takes off her helmet and rushes over to me, opening her arms for a hug. Amanda and Farren watch as she embraces me. Warm tingles spread over my body, and for the first time since the separation, I realize how much I missed her.

Amanda crosses her arms, smiling, as Leeyah lets me go. She says nothing. Right now we have Stratton to deal with. The Influencer groans as Farren and Stanley hike him up.

Leeyah nods to the subway entrance. "We need to interrogate him. Jax, Kaylin, Ava, and Envee, the four of you will need to ensure that he doesn't use his Push on my people."

"No problem," Envee says, rocking back and forth on her feet.

Leeyah's back to business. Farren and Caiden carry Stratton down the stairs while Stanley trails close behind. The subway tunnels are dark, but it's clear that Leeyah has navigated them before. She turns on a flashlight and guides us past a station as rats scurry out of the way, their hollow footfalls echoing off the walls. Stratton groans. Maybe he has a rat phobia. I hope that he does.

Our combined teams walk in silence past the station and then down some tracks, stepping over old food containers, abandoned shoes, puddles of water, and even a human skeleton complete with gnawed bones. It's no wonder the Harvesters don't like this place.

At last, Leeyah leads us to another smaller abandoned station that's covered in dust-loaded cobwebs. She motions to a row of yellow chairs that sit under an advertisement for some sort of fizzy drink. Farren and Stanley sit, forcing Stratton to sit between them.

"Jax," she says, nodding him, "please relieve Stanley of this duty. I want only those who aren't affected by Stratton's Pushes to handle him right now. The rest of us will ask him questions. I see that he's waking."

"I'm staying," Caiden says flatly. "There's no way I'm leaving my team down here alone with that *thing*."

"You should go, Caiden," Jax insists. "He got to you before."

Caiden shakes his head and folds his arms. He's stubborn and won't budge.

"I'll watch his awareness," I tell Jax.

Jax sighs and rolls his eyes. "Fine."

Ava, Envee, and I step to the front of the group while Leeyah directs her fighters to place their guns under another row of chairs just in case Stratton uses his Push. My heart leaps into my throat as Stratton lifts his head from his chest and opens his eyes. They appear even more soulless than before in the dim light cast by the weak beam of the flashlight Leeyah still holds.

"Mr. Stratton?" she says. "We have some questions for you. Do not try to use your Push on me. It won't work. But I'm sure you already know that."

"You can just call me Leo." Stratton speaks without emotion as he flicks his gaze over the surrounding fighters. No one speaks. Then his attention falls on me. He stares at me for the longest second of my life, his expression unreadable. "The Vernon Society changed it to Jace when they found and took me at the age of ten. They didn't want the other groups to track me down. The Society's been negotiating with them enough lately, trying to keep them out of their territory. If the other groups know which Influencers they have, things might not go so well. I suppose you want to know my sob story now?"

"We all have one," Jax says.

Stratton turns a look of pure hatred on Jax. "I had a *wonderful* childhood as a young Influencer in your Society." For the first time, pain tightens Leo's features, betraying a tortured past.

"It's not *my* Society," Jax snaps.

"You're naïve," Leo tells him. His mouth curls up into a grin, but there's no joy in it.

Jax shifts in his chair. Stratton doesn't need to use a Push to make him uncomfortable. He has words, and he's wielding them well, but Leeyah's right that she needs the strongest people she has to control him.

Jax swallows, ready to take the peacekeeper approach. "Look, I understand what it's like to deal with Influencer powers at a young age. I was reckless, and it got my parents captured by the Society. It's because of them that they're—"

"You don't have an ability like mine!" Stratton pulls against their grasps, but Farren and Jax keep him in the chair. "You haven't seen what I have and you accuse *me* of being a monster."

"That's because you *are* one," I say.

"You don't know me."

"Why do you do what you do?" Jax asks.

Stratton tries to shrug. "What choice do I have? It was work for them or die."

"You could have escaped."

"I was *ten* when they took me in. I was hungry, so I Influenced Harvesters away from their tower for food. Don't tell me you wouldn't have done the same."

Jax looks to me, silently asking me to keep squeezing information out of Stratton. He must know the inner workings of the Society almost as well as Laney and Talik, but he isn't going to give it up easily. We have to use his pain to get him to talk. It feels fitting.

"But you could have left later," I say. "After they started trusting you."

Stratton fixes me in his glare. "They never did."

"And then you started killing for them," Farren adds, fists balled.

"Go ahead. Keep calling me a monster," Stratton says.

His words echo off the subway tunnels, threatening to haunt them forever. Jax twitches his mouth like he wants to say something, but then he regains his composure. It can't be easy for him, knowing he's like Stratton in a way. The thought of his parents molding Stratton into this must also torment him.

"Why didn't you try to escape after they made you start killing?" Leeyah asks him. "How could you live with what they were forcing you to do?" Emotion tightens her voice. Stratton's words are causing her pain, too. There must be a story behind her that I haven't learned yet.

"Just tell us," Jax insists. "I can tell that you want to tell someone about it, but can't make yourself. You keep giving us hints, but you're not spilling."

"Why would it matter, Mr. Psychologist?" Stratton snaps.

"Because you don't *have* to keep killing for them."

"He's not going to change," Farren says, tightening his grip on Stratton's arm.

"You're with fellow Influencers," Jax says.

"But do you kill?" Stratton asks. "Does your soul erode each time you use your ability?"

Jax swallows. Leeyah shifts around as if she wants to escape, but she stays.

"We can all kill," I say, my mouth dry. "I've done it."

Ava gulps. "And so have I."

Stratton stays silent, eyeing the floor. "Do you do it almost every day?"

"If we were forced to work for a sector group like the Society, we probably would," Leeyah admits.

"Why should I talk to you?" Stratton asks. He turns his hatred on Jax. "People just pretend they care about you until a better thing comes along."

"But I thought the Society *didn't* care about you," I say.

Stratton continues to glare at Jax. "You were smart to get away from your parents. They treated me great for a few months when they got elected, but the second Neira came along with news of you and Kaylin, guess what?"

Jax struggles to speak. "They brushed you aside."

"You don't have a family," Stratton says. "None of us do. We're born to be used."

I search the others for any signs of a Push. The fighters remain at attention, waiting for Stratton to make a move. Amanda shrugs at me. Caiden tightens his stance. The air remains musty, but thin enough to breathe. Other than the darkness cast by the old station, there's no dread in the air. He's not trying to escape.

"But family is who you choose," Jax says. "We Influencers have to stick together."

"You can't *make* someone care about you," Stratton says. "Even if you try to be the best Influencer to get them back. Even with Neira expanding your reach and making you more deadly than you could imagine. Try to impress them, and you turn dark, and there's nothing left inside of you. Family is a sham."

Silence falls over us. Leeyah opens her trembling mouth to say something, but then she regains her composure. She watches as Stratton leans back in his seat, the posture of someone who's giving up. The Influencer before us is a victim. He's what Jax and I might have become if the Magnus Order had kept us. What sits before me is my biggest fear.

Jax swallows again. "I know an apology for what happened to you wouldn't be enough—"

"Don't give this guy an ounce of sympathy," Farren interrupts. "He made innocent people blow themselves up. He made Stanley kill one of our fighters and now the guy's going to live with that for the rest of his life." He looks at Stratton. "I'll shoot him myself. He's a danger to all of us. The moment we give him an inch is the moment he'll turn on us. He said it himself. There's no soul left in him."

I back away, shocked that Farren would do such a thing, but Farren stands and motions with his hand for a weapon. Stanley steps forward, giving him a pistol.

Stratton remains calm, eyeing the ceiling.

"No," I say, stepping forward. "Laney and Talik could have made any of us like this. Any Influencer can be forced to become a killer."

"Kaylin," Amanda grabs my arm, "we can't trust him. Someone without a soul will turn on us for his own benefit. He's not capable of remorse anymore."

She doesn't understand. I blink as the image of those bloody, barely-alive bullies in the cafeteria return to me, the bodies outside the ranger station, the Harvesters in Lost Souls who turned on each other. Amanda had no hand in those deaths and can't imagine what it's like. I wrench my arm from her grasp.

"You've never had someone try to use you for an ability you didn't ask for," I say.

"It's still not right," Caiden mutters.

Breece steps forward from the crowd her face contorted in anger. "Stratton's Push killed my brother two months ago. I'm with Farren on this one."

My stomach churns. Farren tightens his grasp around the pistol. Now I understand Breece's change in attitude when Stratton came around. It seems that Jax and I are the only ones who can see the truth. If anyone else does, they're too afraid to speak up. I look to Leeyah, but indecision plagues her as she looks to everyone else for a vote.

"Kill him," one of the Protectors says. "I remember that Push."

"Farren…" I protest. I don't want to watch him carry out the execution.

He looks to me. "Kay, I know this is hard for you, but Stratton's admitted that he's beyond our help."

Stratton growls and swings his free hand at Jax. He strikes him in the shoulder, forcing him to loosen his grip. Jax shoots up from the seat, but it's too late. Stratton seizes the pistol from Farren.

"Back away," Stratton says, an eerie calm in his words. He raises the pistol not at us, but at the vulnerable space under his chin. He closes his eyes, serene, as he curls his finger around the trigger.

Amanda pulls me back just as I realize what's about to happen, but Jax grabs and pulls Stratton's hand, pointing the pistol at the ceiling just as he fires.

16

TESTED

STRATTON BREATHES OUT, confined once again to the chair. Jax and Stanley hold him down, not saying a word to each other or to anyone else. Farren paces, biting his lip. The pistol remains on the floor and the air still smells of the single gunshot that Stratton meant to end his life with.

The only reason Stratton isn't dead yet is the shock that encompasses the rest of us. Amanda looks at me and lifts one eyebrow, then turns her attention back to Stratton.

"His gunshot might have alerted someone nearby that we're in this tunnel," Leeyah says. "Breece, Nance, make sure the tunnel is secure." She waves them in opposite directions. I watch as the two fighters take their teams away from the area, splitting into two groups. Both teams wander into the darkness on either side of the tunnel.

Leeyah turns her attention to Stratton, who's staring at the dusty floor. So far, he's not trying to use his Push. I'm getting the sense that once away from the Vernon Society, he never meant to use it on us.

"Can I speak to him?" I ask Leeyah. Until now, I've never asked anyone other than Amanda whether or not I could do anything, but it feels right to have her input.

"I doubt he'll have anything useful to say," Caiden says.

Leeyah lifts her fingers to her chin to think. "He's restrained and I've sent away most of the fighters," she says hesitantly.

Amanda sends me a glare. "Kaylin doesn't need to talk to him."

"Don't go back to this again," I say. "It's important. This could have been any of us."

It's obvious that I've hit the right buttons. Amanda doesn't resist when Ava takes her arm and guides her away.

"So what are we going to do?" Envee asks, shifting uncomfortably at my words. The two of them must be mulling that over. All of us, without exception, could have been used to kill. Stratton just happened to have an ability very fine-tuned for it.

"Go ahead," Leeyah tells me.

A strange feeling fills my chest as I take a step toward our enemy. "You can make things better," I say, trying to channel Ava's words. "We Influencers have the power to affect the world around us and make reality a better place. Leo, you can work to make things right now that you're away from Neira and the Vernon Society. You don't have to impress Laney and Talik anymore. Out here, we're a family."

Stratton doesn't look up at me at first. But then he lifts his head and meets my gaze. Is there anyone in there?

"You've seen what I am," he mutters, defeated. "And you refused to let me make the world a better place by taking myself out of it. If the Society finds me again, they'll force me to kill."

"They're going to do that to all of us," I tell him. Everyone remains silent, letting me be in charge. The feeling is surreal. "If they catch any of us Influencers, we'll be ordered to kill." I debate on telling Stratton about my own experiences and decide that would be going too far. "You can get back at the Vernon Society by helping us make the world into something they don't want."

Farren shakes his head in disgust. It almost makes me stop. "He has no right to join us," Farren argues. "What would Breece think about that?" He levels a glare at me that I've never seen before, showing me a different side of him that turns my stomach.

"Give him a chance," I say. "Stratton is a victim."

"Maybe we should," Jax agrees. "I know what it's like to be made to do things that I don't want to do."

"You have to be kidding me," Farren grumbles, turning his back on all of us.

"Farren. Listen," I plea, but he's walking away. The silence is somehow worse than his anger. My chest tightens, but we have a mission here. What if Stratton has the key to stopping the Vernon Society?

"So you've changed your minds," Stratton says. He's more curious than afraid. The scary calm is still there. "You won't let me die."

Jax swallows. "All of us are connected. Me, you, Kay, even Caiden and Farren over there and the guards in the tunnels. We're all one consciousness split into multiple parts. Surely you've noticed that as an Influencer. You might not have had a name for it, but that's what it is. Anyone in that web has a chance for redemption. That includes you. It was the Society who killed those people, not you, no matter what they chose to have you believe. Even Neira might get the chance to redeem herself, given enough time. But it's *your* choice. There's a family waiting for you if you would only accept it. There are people who understand you."

"He's already made his choice!" Farren shouts back to us.

Stratton exhales and keeps his gaze on the floor. "That's not how things work."

"They *can* work that way," Jax insists. "It's a matter of meeting the right people. The Society wants you to feel this way. Do you want to let them win?"

Stratton snaps his gaze up at Jax. Jax hit a nerve.

"Just let him die!" Farren yells.

"I agree," Amanda says. "We've seen the things he can make people do. He turns them into zombies and makes them into killing machines. I can forgive a child forced into that situation, but I cannot forgive an adult who's made no attempts to escape. You heard him, he's done this to impress the Society."

"Everything's clear," Breece says from behind us, but she sounds a million miles away.

Jax stares her down with a calm but intent gaze. "I did the same," he says. "It was for a different purpose, but it's a mistake I've made as well."

"Then why don't we open our arms and let him in?" Amanda asks, doing that with an air of sarcasm.

"What a great idea," Caiden adds, sarcasm heavy in his voice. "Let someone with a vested interest in impressing the Vernon Society into our ranks. Someone who has lost all capability to feel remorse for what he's done, and who would much rather stay that way than face up to it."

"Come on," I urge, knowing that Caiden will be the last one to accept Stratton. "It's obvious that he doesn't want to fight us anymore. If he could, he would have. Why don't we ask Breece for her opinion again?" She has much more of a stake in this than me. No Influencer abilities grace or curse her, but losing her brother gives her a lot of say in this conversation.

But I hope that we can keep Stratton, that we can find a way to stop the Society.

Breece walks into the crowd. Everyone parts for her. "Let me think." Our words have been loud enough to reach her even as she walked up the tracks.

Leeyah places her hand on the fighter's back. "What do you say?" There's no pressure in the question that I can detect.

The look in Stratton's eyes has changed as he waits. Now they're hungry for something. Acceptance? No...maybe it was vengeance.

Breece takes her time. I begin to wonder if I've put too much pressure on her by asking her opinion again, but then she speaks.

"Maybe we should give him *one* chance. He does know the Society leadership well, and may be able to tell us what moves they'll make. I'm all for keeping him guarded at all times until he proves that we can trust him—and it'll take a long time—but if Stratton can dedicate himself to saving lives rather than taking them, then maybe he should join us."

My mouth falls open. Amanda's does the same. Ava looks at Envee and back at Stratton. Surprise even crosses Jax's face. Forgiveness isn't something I've seen often in Lost Souls or anywhere else. Leeyah's given her fighters a different atmosphere than anyone else I've ever met. She's infected Breece with it, and perhaps the other Protectors as well.

No one protests her decision, not even Farren, who continues to pace at the back of the group. His anger keeps me tense.

Stratton shifts, but does not rise from his seat. "I agree. I'll work with you, and we'll see how things go from there. Shall we?"

"Spoken without an ounce of remorse," Amanda says.

"I'm going to make things right," Stratton insists, coming to life and fixing her with his dark gaze.

"You almost did," Caiden reminds him, "by taking yourself out of this world."

Stratton ignores him. "I want to see the Society fall. If you're going to force me to live, then I want to see them as ruined as I am."

"That's a start," Jax says. "Maybe you'll begin to see the light."

Stratton looks at him as if he's crazy. This is going to be a long process. "I know what you want. You need help to take down the Society."

"We want Influencers to be free," Jax tells him. "Why else would we want to do that? It doesn't have to be this way for us. Help us reach that future."

"Fine," Stratton agrees.

"We need to keep him on a leash," Farren insists, pushing through the crowd. "A very, *very* short leash." He steps between me and Stratton, staring him down.

"Then he can stay close to his enemies and use his Push when we're not watching," Caiden adds.

"Then we have an agreement," Leeyah says, ignoring him, the corner of her mouth curling up into a smile. She pats me on the shoulder. "Leo's gotten close to Laney and Talik over these past months and will no doubt have valuable information for us. Shall we get moving? And yes, those of us who are not affected by Pushes need to keep a close watch on Leo."

Her calmness and confidence has its desired effect. Our fighters all gather their weapons—hesitantly at first—while Jax and Stanley help Stratton stand. I wait for the cloud of darkness and despair to sweep over our group, but the air remains chilly and otherwise clear. He's not trying to harm us anymore.

"Great work, Kaylin," Ava says beside me. For the first time all day, she gives me a real smile. "I couldn't have said it better myself."

"Thanks," I manage. "Do you think we got to him?"

"I think that we did."

"Farren and I are in for an argument later," I say, hoping for advice. If anyone will have it for me, it will be Ava.

Sadness fills her deep brown eyes. Thoughts of Maddux must be swirling through her head. "It will pass," she says, staring at the tunnel ahead as we walk.

I wait for Farren to fall in beside me, but he walks ahead, behind Jax and Stanley and Stratton, not looking back to check on me once. I want to think Farren's just trying to keep a barrier between me and Stratton, but his shoulders remain elevated, betraying his tension and anger.

The subway tunnels remain dead as flashlight beams swing, illuminating garbage, fleeing rats, and green trash cans with peeling paint. We pass an intersection where tracks curve and meet, faded warning signs on the walls that point to another station. The letters are no longer legible.

Leeyah doesn't talk much as we walk. Everyone remains silent, including Farren and Amanda. Our footsteps scrape over dust and concrete. It seems we're taking a mostly underground route back to the research facility. It's a smart idea, and clearly one that the Protectors have used before.

At last, Leeyah waves us toward another set of stairs. Flashlights click off as pale sunlight pours down the steps, showing us the way. Stratton lets out a breath. Even Farren's shoulders slump as he releases some tension. Just getting out of the tunnels is calming everyone's nerves.

Blinking, I emerge into the sunlight beside Amanda and Ava. My eyes adjust and I realize we're two streets over from the research facility. I recognize the stack of crates in front of an old florist shop with the dusty windows and the unreadable white text on the glass.

We're close to the hideout, and we're bringing Stratton into it. A sense of dread settles over me as I think about that, and I shake my head as we continue to walk. The feeling doesn't go away. The exhaustion of everyone fills the air. I'm surrounded by sleepy consciousness.

That's not right.

I face Amanda. "Does something feel off?"

She blinks, almost as if she's in a mild trance.

"Amanda!"

"Huh?" she asks.

I spot movement ahead of us.

"Harvesters!" Farren shouts, lifting his weapon.

Everyone up front scrambles. People jostle against each other. Stratton's using his Push.

Amanda grabs my arm as the alley in front of us fills with two dozen dirty bodies carrying boards, glass bottles, and other blunt objects. These Harvesters are different than the ones we encountered earlier. None of them speak or react to the guns pointing at them. Rather, they continue to shuffle forward like zombies, eyes blank and dead. I send out my awareness, but detect dulled, sleeping consciousness coming from the mass. This is something I've sensed before, back at Talas, when Stratton was using his Push to make innocents detonate themselves.

"He's trying to escape!" I shout, jumping to see over those in front of me.

Stanley has his gun raised at the approaching Harvesters. Jax backs up, weaponless, allowing Farren to jump forward and take his place. Stratton's nowhere to be found...until I look up and spot movement shuffling toward the top of a brick apartment building. He climbs a service ladder, his leg knocking off an ancient plant pot on a balcony as he disappears over the rooftop.

17

MOMENTUM

"THERE HE GOES!" Caiden shouts, pointing at the now empty ladder. "Handle the Harvesters. We're going after that piece of crap."

Shouting at him to wait isn't an option right now. The Harvesters close in, blunt weapons ready. Without closing my eyes this time, I send my awareness out to them. Envee tugs on my shirt sleeve, ready to go, and amplifies my Push beyond the next couple of streets. My consciousness sweeps outward, blanketing the streets, but I'm quick to notice that beyond our small area, the Harvesters are absent.

Stratton only sent this small group at us—a distraction, not an attack.

Zeroing back in on the two dozen Harvesters, I enfold them with feelings of forgiveness and calm as I close my eyes. The small crowd slows and disperses away from us. I could use my Push to do the same for the Protectors so they don't open fire, but there's no need. No one does.

"I guess you didn't need me, then?" Envee asks, making me open my eyes.

I face her. "Guess not. There weren't a lot of them."

The alley ahead is now free of Harvesters, but Farren, Caiden, and a few of the Protectors are gone. And so is Stratton.

"Fan out," Leeyah orders. "We need to find him, but do not shoot. We need him alive. Kaylin, Jax, we need the two of you to stay sharp."

We split into two groups. I stay with Leeyah, Envee, and Ava as Jax heads off with the other group, promising to protect them from Stratton's Push if needed. I know he's capable of defending himself and his party, but worry sweeps over me at the thought of him leaving.

Leeyah and Nance guide us through alley after alley, but there's no sign of Stratton anywhere. She has Nance climb several ladders to peek at rooftops, but every time he looks down at us and shakes his head. I feel no sense of dread or despair, even as I try with Envee's help to send my awareness out into our surroundings. Stratton isn't trying to use his Push. The overwhelming sense that he's gone soft on us hits me. Perhaps he hadn't wanted to kill us at all, but like Laney, still has a bit of humanity left in him.

At last, we meet back up Breece's team in another alley.

"He seems to have fled the area," Breece reports. "We've seen no sign of him."

"I agree," Jax says when Leeyah looks at him.

Farren and Caiden push out from behind Jax, Caiden giving Jax a shove as he does so. Both of their faces are flushed with the effort of trying to chase down Leo. Even without my awareness, I can tell the two of them are upset with me and Jax, and now rightly so.

Ava clears her throat. "We can't act like children right now."

"We're acting like people who've just had a high-profile prisoner escape," Caiden corrects. "One who now knows what area the Protectors are using to hide."

"Then we need to pull back to the facility," Leeyah says. "He does not know where it is, so that's fortunate. Nance, Breece, lead the way, and everyone needs to remain quiet."

Amanda glares at me as we walk, but it's a protective glare. That instinct is still alive and well in her, despite me going off on my own several times now. A part of me is glad to see it, but Farren's doing the same thing to me, and that's different.

We take a different route to the research facility. It adds several minutes of walking, but we arrive and enter the empty building. Filing through the lobby, we pass the offices. The air thickens with tension as Leeyah leads us to a small auditorium with a large white screen at the front and numerous scattered chairs sprawled about. This room was likely once used for VeRx's scientific presentations and findings. Pieces of ceiling tiles have fallen onto the moldy seats, but at least the area is dry. It's dark except for some battery-powered lanterns that the Protectors get out, but I can't help but feel there's a spotlight on me and Jax.

I separate from Amanda and Farren, who still give me the cold shoulder. Jax and I need to stand together for this. Ava joins us, though Envee stands back. She didn't have anything to do with the decision to let Stratton live. I'm jealous that she can stand out of this and still be a kid.

But at least Leeyah is here. She gives me an encouraging smile as I divert my gaze from Farren. None of us sit on the old seats. Rather, we stand near the dusty stage and the projector that's no longer in use.

"As we all know," Leeyah says, "Stratton has gotten away from us, but the game may not be over yet. In fact, this all might be a good thing. I don't believe that Stratton wanted to harm us. If he had, he would have attacked our fighters rather than sent a distraction."

Leeyah and I think the same, then. Caiden opens his mouth like he wants to say something, but it seems his tactical mind can't come up with another explanation. Stratton could have done much worse than diverting us with some easy Harvesters, but chose instead to flee.

"He still might go back to the Vernon Society," Farren says. "He has nothing else."

"But he doesn't *have* to go back," I say. It's odd for Farren to say that, considering that he once had to work for the Magnus Order to keep his family safe. He knew what that was like. "Stratton didn't say that they have his relatives or anything. As long as he stays free, there's a chance they won't find him again. And Leeyah's right that he didn't want to hurt us anymore. He just wanted to get away."

Farren's glare softens. Now that emotions are dying down, we can all reason more logically. Maybe I'll be able to talk to him once this is over.

But Leeyah is all business right now. She places her hand on my shoulder and squeezes, reassuring me. "Stratton may be gone, but Kay is right that he may not head back to the Vernon Society. This means the Society may have lost one of its most powerful weapons to use against us. In addition, we've caused a lot of chaos in the last few days that may also give us an advantage. With the help of Jax, Kay, and these other wonderful Influencers, we may be able to free this sector from the Vernon Society's control. These experienced Resistance fighters have already helped to take down one sector group, and I'm confident they can do it again."

Leeyah glances at Jax, but he shifts from foot to foot and bumps into a moldy chair. "Those...those are my parents we're talking about. The Magnus Order was different."

"We will not kill them," Leeyah assures him. I'm sure that she's telling the truth. "I only want to break their organization apart. Laney is still my sister, and I'm certain there's still some good in her. Humanity's Protectors are not like the sector groups that we've vowed to keep under control. We only kill if we must."

Leeyah's hand trembles as she speaks. There's emotion that she's trying to hide, and I can't put my finger on it. She lets go of my shoulder as if afraid I'll detect it. It seems that every time she talks about her sister she goes to a dark place. I can't imagine what kind of past they had together.

"I agree," I add. "We can help. Jax?"

"So long as we don't kill them." He speaks with calm, but his gaze is intense as he eyes Leeyah. "We don't kill them, no matter what."

Leeyah instructs us all to take a break, get our bearings, and go get a bite to eat. We all file out of the auditorium while she hangs back with Caiden, Breece, and Nance. Jax also walks beside her. I know why he's hanging around her. He needs every assurance he can get that Leeyah won't harm his parents. That's understandable. The five of them begin a low, hushed conversation as I file out the door with Amanda, who smiles at me. It's forced, but that makes me feel a lot better.

"I still worry about you," Amanda says, patting me on the back.

"I know you do, and I'm sorry about what happened." We turn the corner to the small cafeteria, already full of people grabbing food. Other Protectors move into the side offices, sitting to eat and calm their minds. It's been a stressful morning, and we can't go on until we take a break. Resting our minds is just as important as resting our bodies.

"I'm not an Influencer, so I didn't have much say in that conversation," Amanda says. "Maybe I should've kept my mouth shut."

"But Stratton got away," I point out. "That was my fault."

"I wasn't thinking." Amanda gets in line for the small buffet of leftovers the Protectors are setting on a long table. "All I could think about was not letting that scumbag anywhere near you."

"And I appreciate it," I say, grabbing a plate.

I feel the tingly warmth before she appears.

"So, you're Amanda?" Leeyah asks from behind us.

Amanda smiles at Leeyah and shuffles down the table to let her access the grub. "Yep. Me and Kay have been sticking together for the past several years. You could say I took care of her for that time. She was in good hands with me, and still is."

"Amanda!" I hiss. "I'm not eleven anymore."

Leeyah grins. "Well, it looks like you did a fine job. I'm glad that Kay had someone like you looking out for her. Hardly a day passed when I didn't worry."

"Had?" Amanda echoes half-jokingly, but the line continues to move and Leeyah vanishes with a plate of macaroni salad in tow.

"Don't worry," I say. "You're not going anywhere. You just don't have to take care of me like you used to anymore."

I wait for Amanda to protest, but instead, she nods. "I guess you have grown up, Kay."

"Thanks. I'm glad you're meeting new people, too. And flirting with the guys."

I spot Farren wandering down the hall, away from everyone else. He has no plate in his hands. Hoping that Amanda understands, I follow him into the quiet. Farren doesn't hear me, but continues into the auditorium, which is now empty of tired, stressed bodies.

I stand in the doorway, unsure of whether to continue. "Farren?"

He whirls and faces me, deep brown eyes locking with mine. My heart races and I suck in a breath. Though sunburned and tired, Farren looks just as amazing as ever, and I have to make things right.

"I'm sorry," I say. "I thought we could save Leo, that maybe he was like me and didn't really want to kill, even if he says there's nothing else for him. I saw what would have happened to me had the Magnus Order kept me. Jax and I really thought that bringing him in for questioning was the right thing to do. We messed up, and I want to apologize for the two of us."

His gaze softens. "Kay, I shouldn't have yelled at you like that. You were under stress, and it wasn't right."

That's my invitation to enter the room, so I do and close the door behind me. My heart races as I near Farren, watching as a smile teases the corner of his lips. His shoulders are still elevated with tension, but with each breath he takes, they lower just a little more.

"But Stratton is dangerous, and you, Amanda, and Caiden all had a point," I continue. "I guess we Influencers have to see things differently than everyone else. We know what it's like to get used or have people want to use us. I still think giving him the chance to redeem himself was the right thing to do."

"And I don't know that?" Farren asks. "Maybe I should have had a bit more sympathy for Leo, but you made me forget that. I was so worried that he'd hurt you that there was no way I could let him live."

"You and Amanda were a team then. And Leo wasn't going to hurt me. The Society wants me and Jax too much for that. Of course, he might not be with them anymore."

Farren steps over to me and takes my wrists, sliding his thumbs up and down my forearm. Though my long sleeved shirt prevents skin on skin, his touch is no less magical. "When you left in the FlexViper with that monster a few days ago, it nearly killed me. I came here to help you, not put you in more danger." Pain fills his eyes. "You were the only thing I could think about on the way to Seattle. Nothing was going to stop me from reaching you again. All I could think about was what the Vernon Society would make you do. I didn't show it well back in the subway, but I didn't know what else to do at the time."

I want to kiss away that pain I helped to cause. "I'm glad you're here. I'm still trying to wrap my mind around it all."

"Well," he says with a grin, "wrap your mind around this."

Farren leans down, and I barely have time to study his incoming lips before ours meet. I stand on my tiptoes, pressing into his kiss as our hearts race with each other. He tastes salty, but still somehow amazingly sweet. We drag our embrace out for as long as we can before we part and gasp for breath.

"That," he says, "was worth everything we had to deal with this morning."

I smile. "Agreed."

"You know, I like your mother," Farren says. "I think these Protectors have a chance to take down the Vernon Society. Now that we have Caiden working with her, they might never be able to use and abuse Influencers ever again."

"This is hard on Jax," I say, heart going out to him. I don't have to say the rest. Soon, he's going to help plan an attack that might even hurt the parents he's been searching for most of his life. But Leeyah and the Protectors will need his leadership skills and his abilities.

"But if we don't stop the Society, they'll keep coming after both of you," Farren reasons. "I'm with the Protectors, and will be every step of the way. With Envee and Ava, you have a chance."

Even with his block implant, I can feel that he means every word. It's there in his eyes. Farren would die for me. The thought sends an unidentifiable feeling through my being.

I open my mouth to say something, anything, when the door to the auditorium bursts open and Leeyah stands in the doorway, every trace of her casual lunch conversation gone.

"It's time," she says. "We need to plan this attack, because I have a feeling we're only going to get one shot at it."

18

BEWARE

MORNING COMES EARLY and without mercy. I scarcely have time to wake and get out of bed at four-thirty before someone knocks on the door to my room.

"Kaylin?" Jax calls.

"I'm up," I say, scrambling to put on the black vest and the black pants Leeyah left out for me. Sleeping hasn't been easy, and it's a struggle to blink the tiredness from my eyes. But as I dress, the fatigue flees to be replaced by a now-familiar sense of dread.

We're taking on the Vernon Society today. Leeyah believes that the best time to attack isn't the dead of night, but the wee hours of the morning when their guards and Influencers will be at their most exhausted.

I open the door. Jax has donned a black vest that matches mine and the same dark, long-sleeved shirt that I now wear. He smiles at me like everything's going to be fine, but I can see the anguish and conflict underneath his calm façade.

"Leeyah's already awake and rallying everyone," he tells me. "They're meeting in the auditorium."

The thought of getting to see Farren and Amanda and Ava propels me to the large space. Many of the Protectors have already gathered there. Leeyah smiles at me as I enter. Envee paces, also in black and ready to move. I envy her amount of energy. We Influencers can rely on her to amplify our Pushes on the Vernon Society. It's our best bet to avoid having to hurt or kill Laney and Talik.

"We're waiting for scouts to return before we move," Caiden says to me with a nod. He paces up and down a row of seats. "Staking out the surrounding city is necessary before we move toward the Vernon Society."

"What about Neira?" Farren asks, appearing out of the semi-dark to stand beside Caiden.

My heart flutters at the sight of him. He's had time to clean up and for the first time, I see how great he looks in black. With a grin, Farren nods a greeting a me.

"She may or may not have Stratton by her side," Caiden says. "That's a situation we'll need to monitor as we go."

"We don't know how many Influencers she can handle at once," Ava adds. "It's my hope that we can overwhelm her."

Our plan is to disable the Society's fighters as much as possible before entering the tower and making our way to the top floor of the building to capture Laney and Talik. Our hope is that Stratton has not re-joined them already, but I sense that after he escaped, he likely won't unless re-captured. Leeyah believes we need to strike before they get him back. Neira might be able to interrupt our Pushes, but without Stratton there to stop the Protectors, we stand a chance at reaching the top floor.

A few more minutes pass as we discuss the plan again. Farren wraps an arm around my waist, pulling me close. Amanda gives him a glare, but I'm glad to see it. We're all together, and Breece's positive attitude is infectious as she helps Leeyah divide the Protectors into three teams.

The auditorium door opens and a group of scouts, all young men and women dressed in black, as we are, step into the room.

"Leeyah, the streets are clear of Harvesters," a young guy reports.

"The entire city has been emptied," his partner, a woman in her twenties, adds. "We spotted a mass exodus of them leaving through the city's western border. The other scouts haven't reported back yet, but I can imagine that the same may be happening through the entire area."

Leeyah stands near one of the battery-powered lanterns, appearing to think. "That tells us the Vernon Society expects us to launch an attack," she says. "They must have used their Influencers to eliminate any complications they may have...and to eliminate one weapon we could've used against them."

"So they must have more Influencers left than just Neira," Ava reasons. "How else could they have cleared the city?"

A heavy silence falls over the room. Farren's grip around my waist tightens. If Stratton and Neira are together again, it would mean that taking down the Society would once again become impossible.

"Not necessarily," Leeyah says. "The Society has been collecting Influencers for years, and some of them are talented. The intelligence the Protectors gathered has told us they have maybe a half dozen Influencers in their ranks. This does not sound like Stratton's doing. More like Neira's, perhaps, along with other Influencers."

Jax clears his throat. "We don't know for certain." He's scared again, and I can see it in the way he shifts from leg to leg. There's a part of him that doesn't want to have anything to do with this attack.

"Yes, I agree. We don't know," Leeyah says.

Caiden steps in front of Farren, pushing against the seats in front of him to go around us. "There's too much risk in this mission. There are too many unknown variables."

"But there's a chance that Stratton isn't back with them yet," I add. Caiden still isn't happy with me about convincing everyone not to kill him. He hasn't spoken to me since yesterday.

"Kaylin has a point," Amanda says. "We may have opened up an opportunity simply by sympathizing with Stratton."

It's odd to see her trying to keep me safe less and less. It's as strange as seeing Jax scared and unsure or Farren angry with me. My entire world is changing, and it's not going to become any more stable anytime soon.

"Yes," Leeyah agrees. "We have one chance to move and stop them from taking any more territory, and it's right now." She looks at Breece and Nance, who once again head their own teams. "I will go with Breece's team. I want all the Influencers on Nance's team."

"Kaylin's going to be in the back," Amanda says, glaring at me. "There's no need for her to be at the front, especially with Envee amplifying her Push."

"Agreed," Farren says. Then he faces me. "I'm going with you. I don't want you putting yourself at risk."

There's no arguing with them. I do feel better that we're all going to be together, though disappointed that Breece and Leeyah won't be coming with us.

People could *die* today. The thought invades my head over and over, building pressure inside me, but I breathe out, trying to tell myself it'll all be fine now that Jax can't comfort me. Neither will Amanda. This must be what adulthood feels like. It's not an easy transition.

Leeyah leads us out of the auditorium and into the dark of the early morning. I walk behind Amanda and beside Farren, trying to recall how long it took us to reach the research facility from the Society headquarters. Envee practically skips alongside us as if trying to expend excess energy while Ava and Jax remain quiet. The streets are foggy and eerily silent. Only the occasional scurrying of an animal meets my ears.

"Stay sharp," Ava tells me.

I expand my awareness further outward with each breath. The scouts are right that the Harvesters have left the city, turning it into a giant, silent maze. I only detect the bright consciousnesses of small animals or the occasional dog foraging through the trash, trying to find a bite to eat. There are none of the dulled minds of the Harvesters in the area. There's nothing to work with. Of course, that leaves the Society without any Harvesters to use as well.

"There's no one out here," I whisper.

Ava nods. "I know."

No one speaks as we continue to make our way through the streets, which grow larger and wider. The sky turns dark gray and lightens as the sun begins to rise. Leeyah waves us forward again and again, urging us to hurry. After nearly an hour, an ache creeps into the soles of my feet. Eventually, apartment buildings tower over us, rising into the mist. Damp coolness wraps around me, making me shiver. I fear speaking, as someone might hear our presence in this gloom, but I have a burning question.

"How many in the Vernon Society have block implants?" I ask one of the Protectors, a young woman covered in tattoos.

"They say most of them do," she tells me in a tone that warns me to be quiet.

I guess this sort of tech wasn't going to remain with one sector group. It was bound to get out.

Far ahead, Breece holds up a clenched fist, urging us to stop. She stands in the shadow of two tall buildings and takes a step back, bumping into Leeyah. The mist is already starting to rise, leaving us exposed.

"We're close to the headquarters," Nance explains. "We need to wait for—"

A new sound cuts him off, transporting me back to that day at Talas when I had to leave Farren and Amanda behind—the wind-driven hum of a FlexViper. As I listen, the noise intensifies and a black, smooth shape appears from the mist, almost low enough to clip the buildings.

Farren seizes my arm and pulls me to the edge of the apartment building. A moment later, the world fills with gunfire.

Sparks rise from the pavement as the deafening *pops* continue and our fighters part, taking cover behind trash cans, dumpsters, and anything else that can offer shelter. Bullets ricochet off the rooftops and the balconies above, which offer the only real protection from the deadly rain. Opposite me, Envee covers her ears and screams. A young man falls ahead of us, blood spraying from his chest and then his back as another slug pierces his body. Amanda and Ava smash themselves behind a pile of trash as the FlexViper sails overhead, finishing its attack.

I suck in a breath. The Vernon Society already knows we're approaching.

"Are you okay?" Farren asks.

"Yes. But people are dead," I say.

"It's unfortunate. War always is," he says, running his hand over his hair. "I've seen enough of it."

"Man down!" Caiden shouts from ahead. "I hear more of them approaching! Take cover!"

Another hum, this time louder than before, approaches from the sky. I glimpse two more dark shapes—two more FlexVipers—as Farren pulls me away from the building and into a narrower alley lined with more balconies and old clotheslines. Envee screams again. I glimpse Amanda and Ava leading her into an open doorway and up a stairwell. Jax closes the door, protecting them. Caiden shouts something else and Breece's high-pitched voice follows.

The two new FlexVipers open fire. Bullets spray the street as the vehicles fly over, blasting wind down into the alley and whipping my ponytail against my cheek. Caiden ducks into the alley after us as two more Protectors follow. The FlexVipers sail over and the hum fades, but does not vanish. The three of them are circling back around for another attack.

"Kaylin, you have to try a Push," Farren says, eyeing the balcony above us, our only protection from another attack. "Envee's too terrified to help you right now."

He's right, and I won't be able to coordinate anything with Jax, Ava, or Envee. Terror fills my chest and makes my heart race, driving away all sense of concentration. The pilots might all have block implants, but I breathe out, readying myself anyway. Leeyah's still somewhere ahead on the street, and it's possible that she's hurt, dying, or dead.

"Kaylin, focus," Caiden says, pacing. "Our guns won't do us any good right now."

Closing my eyes, I force my awareness out into the sky. I briefly sense the sharp terror of the other Protectors, scattered around the street and the nearby alleys, and a flash of warmth from where Leeyah's stationed herself toward the front. A mountain of terror lifts from my shoulders, but only for a second. I turn my attention to the sky, to where some terrified birds have taken off from the tops of buildings to escape the metal monsters flying overhead. Pinpoints of the animals' fear race through my web of consciousness, and I zero in on the FlexVipers. From them, I feel nothing. These Vernon Society people do have block implants meant to prevent a Push. There's nothing I can do against them.

Opening my eyes, I shake my head at Caiden. "Block implants," I say. "Does anyone have a block disruptor?"

Farren nods. "Ava gave one to Breece and one to Nance, but the pilots might not be close enough to reach. It's iffy."

I tear away from him as the windy hum of the FlexVipers begins to intensify again. With the rising mist, there's no telling how close they are.

Staying under the balcony, I look around the corner to see that many of the Protectors have ducked out of sight and underneath other balconies—but not all of them. Breece and Leeyah struggle to open an apartment door as other Protectors huddle under cover. There's no doubt that the two of them opted to let their teams take cover first.

Three dark shapes appear overhead as Farren and Caiden take my arms. They pull me back, but not fast enough. One of the FlexVipers opens fire on Leeyah and Breece. Breece lets go of the door and moves herself in front of Leeyah.

"No!" I shout.

Breece jolts and blood spurts as several of the bullets find their mark. Her body jerks back, pressing Leeyah against the wall and out of harm's way.

At the same time, Farren and Caiden shield me under the balcony. The storm continues and a wail rises in my throat, but Farren clamps his free hand over my mouth, urging me to stay quiet.

"There's nothing we can do for her now," he says in my ear. He presses his cheek against mine. "Nothing at all."

19

DEFINING MOMENT

EXISTENCE BLURS AS I let Farren and Caiden pull me through a side door and into the apartment building. Outside, the onslaught continues as those left behind try to take cover. I blink and Breece's jolting body replays in my mind.

"Close the door!" Caiden shouts.

The door slams behind me. I open my eyes to find we're standing in a dark hallway lined with apartments. Many of the doors lay open as past evidence of looters or residents fleeing for their lives. The faint reek of burnt food fills the air. The others are dark shadows standing next to me.

The gunfire dies outside and the hums of the FlexVipers fade, but I know that they're coming around again. I face Caiden. He has the best combat experience out of us all. We need his strategy right now.

Caiden adjusts his backpack. "Those Vipers are coming back, guaranteed," he says. "Now that we've established that the Influencers can't stop them, our best hope is to set a trap. Follow me up the stairs."

The last place I want to go is closer to the FlexVipers, but Farren and I follow Caiden up the dark stairwell past floor after abandoned floor. At last, after my legs begin to quiver with effort, he shoves open a door with a bronze number ten nailed to it. There are no higher floors. Caiden has taken us to the very top. On the other side of the door are more empty apartments and another door labeled *Maintenance Only* that must lead to the roof.

"You're going up there?" I ask when I see Caiden eyeing it.

"It's our best bet to set a trap. Kaylin, stay down here." He faces the three Protectors who have come with us. "I'm going to rig some explosives on the roof. We'll lure the Vipers over by attempting to shoot at them from a window. I can detonate them from below when the Vipers fly over." Caiden pulls off his backpack and throws it on the worn carpet. He unzips it and shuffles through, pulling out a wired black box. The sight of it sends a shudder through me.

"Is there anything I can do to help?" Killing is horrible, but in order to save the others from this siege, we have to use violence. This is the necessary type that Leeyah talked about.

"Hold the detonator," Caiden says, smiling at me. I've never seen him so alive. "Don't press the button until you have my say-so. The rest of you need to find a window that faces the Vipers. Open fire and draw them close, but don't let them hit you. With any luck, they'll fly over the building." He nods to me. He doesn't need to explain what to do from there.

Caiden shoots the lock off the maintenance door and opens it, revealing a rusty ladder. With the black box in hand, he climbs and pauses as the humming intensifies once again. I hold my breath, waiting for it to fade. This time, no gunfire bursts to life. Everyone must be hiding, trapped.

The humming quiets and Caiden climbs once again. I follow the others into apartment after apartment. Some have been lived in, others not. At last, the Protectors settle on one with a balcony that overlooks the other buildings and faces the rising sun, still tucked behind the buildings. It'll offer the best view, according to one of the fighters, for both them and the incoming Vipers. This apartment also has an abundance of old, but sturdy furniture.

Caiden meets back up with us. "I've planted the explosives near the ventilation system," he says. "They're hidden. The pilots won't see them until it's too late."

"You're fast," Farren remarks, grasping my arm to help me from the floor. We all stand, facing out the window. One of the fighters slides open the balcony door, leaving no barrier between us and the outside.

"Here comes one." Caiden's eyes narrow as he waves us behind the couch.

Two of the Protectors take up positions beside the sliding door. A black shape hums its way towards us like a gigantic, deadly insect. Farren pulls me down and so close to him that our cheeks touch. Caiden fires a shot and the Protectors join in, trying to pelt the Viper with bullets. The humming closes in. Sweat slicks my palms as I eye the detonator. "One chance," I say.

"Take cover!" Caiden orders.

He ducks behind the couch and the Protectors fall to the floor. A second later, a storm of bullets rips into the apartment, jolting the couch and pinging off the outer walls. The humming intensifies and then reaches its peak—

I press the red button on the remote.

A deafening roar sounds above us as the apartment quakes. Horrific screeches fill the air. Dust rains down on us as the ceiling cracks. *Bangs* follow as things strike the roof right above. The light fixture shudders as if in terror.

And the humming has stopped.

Silence falls. The stench of smoke wafts in through the sliding door. Caiden pumps his fist. "Threat neutralized!"

Numb, I drop the detonator that ended the life of the pilot above and stand. The Protectors pick themselves up off the floor as more dust rains from the ceiling. I wonder if it's going to hold, but before I can say anything, more humming fills the air and a dark shadow blocks out the dull sunlight.

And the thing casting the shadow descends into my view.

I hold back a scream. It's another one of the Vipers. We've only destroyed one of them and now the others want revenge. There was no missing that explosion. Glimpsing the dark windshield and a hint of my own reflection, I duck behind the couch and throw myself to the floor, grasping at Farren. He dives on top of me, forming a protective shield as the new Viper opens fire.

Barely able to breathe, I listen to the deafening cacophony of gunfire as the second FlexViper unloads on the tenth floor apartment. All I can do is lie there as Farren lies on top of me, heart racing against my back. The couch lurches with the force of the bullets, threatening to topple back on top of us. Foam explodes as a bullet penetrates the backing and sails over our heads. We're not fully protected.

Caiden shouts an order, but the painful noise of the bullets rips his voice away. An eternity passes, and for the first time I wonder if I'm going to die. At least I'll pass lying up against Farren. Amanda and the others will have a chance to escape, take down the Vernon Society, and make this world a better place.

The gunfire ends.

I take a breath, but Farren remains over me. He breathes against my ear, "Kaylin, are you okay?"

"Move!" Caiden shouts from next to us. "They need to stop because their guns are overheating. Now!"

But then a new round starts up. This one sounds different and doesn't bombard the couch. It's coming from the hallway outside the apartment.

One of the Protectors curses. "It's the other one! I can see it out the bathroom window!"

He's right. From the sounds of it, the third Viper has taken up position on the other side of the apartment building and is firing through the window and into the hallway. The pilots are working together to make sure we have no escape. They want nothing more than to see us in body bags.

Despair settles over the room. They have us trapped. Farren props himself onto his hands, allowing me to breathe. I gaze into his deep brown eyes. He lowers his face to mine for one final kiss. "I'm glad I got to know you, Kaylin."

A sense of calm and peace washes over me. There's nothing either of us can do. "You, too."

A new round of gunfire bursts to life outside the sliding door. We jump and then freeze. Caiden, who kneels beside us, grips the war-torn couch and watches the developments outside. Why isn't he taking cover?

Bullets screech as they strike metal. The couch remains still. There's something different about this attack.

It's not directed at us.

"There's a new FlexViper!" Caiden shouts. "It's attacking the others!"

Curiosity gets the better of me and I rise, Farren beside me, just in time to see sparks flying off our attacker's machine. It lurches, trying to face the new threat, but it's too late. Cracks spider web across the windshield and it shatters, allowing the new FlexViper full access to the pilot. A moment later our attacker lurches away from the building and spirals out of control. The gunfire stops as the new FlexViper turns to deal with the one on the other side of the building. The mysterious pilot who just saved our lives opens fire on the other Viper. I can't see the attack, but it's clear this new pilot is using the element of surprise. These Vernon Society pilots had no clue that someone was coming to back us up.

But who?

"Downstairs!" Caiden orders. "We have a distraction! Everyone! Move!"

Farren and I stand. Couch fuzz litters the floor and broken glass shines everywhere. The three Protectors— unhurt, thankfully—emerge from the apartment's bathroom. We all burst through the door and into the acrid stench of smoke. The unseen FlexViper has torn up the hallway. Bullets lie all over the place, littering the carpet, but now the broken window has nothing on the other side of it but thinning mist and growing sunlight.

Caiden leads the way down the stairwell, which remains empty of threats. I drop the detonator. It's no longer needed and I don't want to hold onto it anymore. One more round of Viper gunfire sounds from outside and then stops. Moments later, there's a crash. The building shakes again, then quiets. The hum of a Viper remains but doesn't move.

"Who helped us?" I ask Farren.

He shakes his head. "Maybe Leeyah's right that Laney still has a heart?"

"She must have ordered this attack," I say. Didn't she realize that Jax might be with this group? I wanted to throw up as the thought hits me. I hope that the pilot knew for sure they weren't firing on Laney's own son when they unloaded on the apartment, or that Laney didn't think Jax would be with us.

He wouldn't fare well after figuring that out.

We reach the bottom floor and Caiden peeks out onto the street. "One of the Vipers crashed two streets over, judging from the biggest plume of smoke," he says. "There are pieces of the one we blew up right outside the door. Be careful not to touch them. They're hot. I can see smoke from the third somewhere behind us. That's the one that just went down."

"What about the other one?" Farren asks, pulling me close to him.

The hum remains. "Whoever helped us is landing," Caiden reports.

Caiden steps out and aims his gun at the perimeter before proceeding. Once he's determined that it's safe, he waves the rest of us out. Farren holds me back and lets the three Protectors go first.

The world is confusion and smoke once we emerge onto the street. Ava and Amanda step out of the opposite building, uncertainty consuming their faces. Envee's jaw drops as she surveys the damage. Jax is very pale and holds his hand over his mouth like he might vomit. There's nothing I can say to him right now.

More Protectors in their black vests emerge from the ravaged buildings, stepping over broken glass. In the middle of it all stands the new FlexViper. Its blades slowly spin to a stop and the wind gusting over the street dies, allowing the Protectors to draw near. Most draw their guns and keep them aimed at the sleek black machine. It has a few bullet holes piercing one side. The other FlexVipers managed to get a few shots off on their attacker.

Leeyah waves the other Protectors back, keeping her gun aimed at the cockpit. She stays ten feet back as both doors lift, giving the FlexViper the appearance of having metal wings. Holding my breath, I watch as nothing happens at first.

Then a lone figure jumps down from the machine, hands raised.

Stratton.

Weapons cock. Farren lets go of me as he and Caiden step forward, raising their guns at Stratton. I wait for the dread and despair to settle over our group, but the atmosphere remains clear.

"Are you kidding me?" Amanda asks. She glares at me and shakes her head, warning me not to try anything stupid.

"What is the meaning of this?" Leeyah asks, keeping her own gun raised.

Stratton doesn't move. He remains under the raised door of the FlexViper as if it will protect him.

"Wait!" Jax shouts, running to stand in front of him. "He just took out two of the Society's FlexVipers for us. If he were here to hurt us, he wouldn't have gone through the trouble of risking his life."

Guns stay pointed at Stratton, and now Jax, but he exudes leadership and paces in front of Stratton, who remains silent. He shifts his dark gaze to Jax first and then to all the others, one by one, sizing up the situation.

"He still sent Harvesters after us after we agreed not to kill him!" Caiden shouts.

"Yes, but he did it to escape, not to hurt us. He knew that we could take care of those Harvesters without violence." The air calms and I realize that Jax is using his Push to deliver a sense of ease to the crowd. Guns lower and shoulders droop.

"Can I speak?" Stratton asks Jax.

"Go ahead," Jax says. "I believe everyone here is interested in what you have to say."

Stratton takes a bold step forward, his hands still raised. "I'm done fighting for the Vernon Society!" he shouts, making his voice echo off the brick of the buildings. "Do I deserve to be forgiven for what I've done? No. But I know how to hurt people, and it's time for the Society to feel that pain. With you, I can do that."

Farren's not having it. Immune from the calming effect of Jax, he steps forward, fists balled. "You say one thing, and then you do another. Listen, everyone, this is a man who has made innocent people sacrifice themselves to kill more people!"

"Please, let's hear him out," Jax tells Farren. "We at least owe him that for saving us back there."

I press forward and stand next to Farren. Grasping his arm, I try to project some peace into him, even though I know it's useless. Amanda glowers and shakes her head at me, but I ignore her.

"Why did you send the Harvesters after us after we agreed to spare your life?" Farren demands.

Stratton doesn't hesitate. "Why stick around with those who don't trust me? With those who wanted to force me to live? I just wanted to...you know, check out. But instead, I thought. There's no sense in dying just to leave the Society to go and make more people like me."

Leeyah nods. Behind her, the body of Breece lies ragged and broken on the pavement. It snaps me back to reality.

If Stratton hadn't attacked, more of us would have died.

"I stole this FlexViper out from under their noses. While I was there, I overheard the pilots talking about what they were going to do. That's when I knew I had to prove myself to you once and for all. I just took down three of their best military pilots." He lets his words hang as their echoes die.

Jax steps forward. "I believe he's earned a bit of trust. He's no longer with the Society, we need to take advantage of this opportunity and strike now." Jax turns to Caiden and then to Farren. "We're not going to turn a blind eye here. We'll be smart about this."

Caiden shakes his head as color flushes his cheeks. Farren drops his shoulders.

"He's proven himself," I insist. "We need him to end this."

"Kaylin, Kaylin," Amanda sighs, shaking her head. "You're too soft for your own good."

"Being soft and smart are two different things," I say, glaring at her.

Ava clears her throat. "Stratton has a lot of potential. He can help us mold reality into something better if he puts his mind to it."

"Maybe," Farren says. "But I'm staying with Kaylin."

Leeyah smiles at me and waves me towards the front of the group. With Breece gone, Nance takes over both parties. "It's best if we stay together from now on," Leeyah says, placing her hand on my back. "Good work, Kaylin."

Stratton stands near the FlexViper, something in the darkness of his eyes. Revenge. Maybe there's a hint of something behind it, something that he doesn't realize still lives. A soul, maybe. It seems that the events of the past several minutes have brought it back from the dead. There's a person in there that I never suspected existed.

"Everyone," I say, "we're almost to the Vernon Society headquarters. We have a chance with Leo on our side. Why don't we end this once and for all?"

20

EXPOSED

THERE ISN'T MUCH time to waste, so we move Breece's body into a nearby apartment and cover her with a fairly clean white blanket we find in a closet. Nance's team brings in two other Protectors' broken bodies and lays them beside her. Leeyah holds back tears as she tells us that if we're able, we'll return and do better for her and the other fallen fighters later.

Outside, Stratton waits, guarded by Caiden and Farren, who still don't trust him. According to Leeyah, he must remain guarded at all times, even as he assists us in our mission.

Taking one last glance at Breece's broken, blanket-covered form, I follow Leeyah and Amanda out of the apartment. Grief will have to come later.

Everyone else waits down in the street. Envee paces, ready to go again now that the gunfire has died down.

Leeyah approaches Stratton. "Tell us what we're up against."

"I'm assuming they've upped their security forces since your last attack on the headquarters," Caiden adds.

"That's true," Stratton confirms, still as a statue. "You may not believe me, but the Vernon Society is more powerful than any of you know. I've also heard talk about them making deals with other groups. I don't know what that's about, but it can't be good. They're not talking to us Influencers as much as before."

"Now you're talking," Caiden says. "Do you have any more intel for us?"

"Not only do they have about seventy-five armed guards around their headquarters, but Miya and Captain Relic have trained them. The Society also has ten Influencers of varying talents and power, headed by Neira. The Vernon Society sends out armed parties of hunters to find and bring in more all the time. I bet you've all heard of that kind of thing?" Stratton asks, as if we should have known this already. Now that he's joined us, his sarcastic attitude is coming back.

"I used to hunt for Influencers," Farren admits. "But I don't anymore."

"Is that how you met your girlfriend?"

Farren flushes.

"Enough," I say. "We need to figure out what to do next."

"It won't be a walk in the park," Stratton says. "The Society is even bigger than that. Hundreds of citizens work with them and live around the headquarters in Society-controlled complexes. The Society also has satellite locations around this sector, just like the Magnus Order used to have. Most of them have an Influencer controlling the people."

"But cutting off the head will deal a critical blow," Caiden reasons. "It worked for us before, and we're going to make it work again."

"This is different from the Magnus Order," Stratton continues. "Laney is obsessed and will do anything to seize more power. She believes that she alone can save the world. I've spent enough time around her to realize that she has a fixation on molding the world to her liking. I wouldn't be surprised if she believes she's a god. Her Royal Highness and Holy Excellency will save us all."

"That's big, coming from you," Farren says.

"Yeah, yeah, I know that I'm not much better," Stratton mutters, not daring to meet Farren's gaze. "But Laney has...problems. She can't even see how she screws up everyone around her."

"That's the definition of insanity," Amanda says. She looks to Ava. "Don't you think?"

Jax backs away from the rest of the group, silent. Leeyah paces and looks around the alleyways as if trying to find an escape. She sucks in a sharp breath. The warm tingles I'm getting from her are frazzled and nervous. Something's eating away at her, and instinctively I reach out and take her black-sleeved arm. "What's wrong?"

Leeyah turns away and faces the building turned morgue. "Laney almost got me killed when we were teenagers."

"She *what*?" Jax cries.

Everyone stays silent, waiting for Leeyah to continue. "Laney was afraid of me when our family found out I was an Influencer. Even after my parents sent me away to work for VeRx, she was looking for ways to fix me and get rid of this terrifying ability I have. Her way of doing that involved working with the corporate police. She thought they could treat me and make me normal."

"Why would she do that?" I ask. "Didn't the corporations, just like the sector groups, wreck everything?"

"Laney didn't know better," Leeyah continues, a deep sadness in her eyes when she turns to face me. "She just wanted to fix me and save me. Instead, she nearly got me killed. I had to use my Push to escape and her boyfriend died as a result. I didn't kill him—another member of the Protectors did—but I froze time and allowed it to happen. Laney failed to fix everything, and as a result something inside her broke. I think it still haunts her."

Froze time? What is she talking about?

Leeyah takes my arms. She's shaking. This conversation isn't an easy one for her to have. "My sister's been trying to ease her pain, but she doesn't know how."

The air hangs heavy with emotion. Jax bites his lip behind Leeyah as she lets me go and turns back to

Stratton, taking a breath to regain her composure. Stratton's dark eyes shimmer with understanding. Jax eyes the concrete and the broken glass. The sense that his world has shattered sweeps over me, and I walk over to him. Right now, my cousin needs me.

"Hey," I say, taking his arm.

At first, he stays silent. I realize that the Protectors are waiting for his input on the situation.

"My mother's insane," Jax says, looking up at Leo. "She needs help. What about my father? Do you have any information about him?"

"Talik has a soul, I think, but he's submissive to Laney and swept up in her ideology, just like the rest of them."

Ava looks to Jax, waiting for him to speak. Even Caiden goes quiet. Jax is still the leader of our band. As if sensing this, he looks at the others in turn. "We need to break apart the Vernon Society," he says. "It's the right thing to do. Maybe we can save my parents before they take things too far and destroy everything around them. There might be a chance." With a glance at Stratton, he nods. "We should move out now that we have this valuable knowledge. Leo, do they have any more FlexVipers on hand?"

Stratton shoots Jax a wicked grin. "Until they can repair the ones that I sabotaged, no."

"Excellent," Caiden says, though refuses to look at Stratton.

Leeyah waves at us to gather and form two lines. "Stay sharp, everyone."

Jax moves to stand behind me while Farren gets in front. Amanda gets waved to the other line, led by Nance, and Leeyah takes the place of Breece. Without her positive attitude, this doesn't feel the same. Caiden walks beside Stratton, gun ready, but Stratton doesn't seem to mind.

Stratton's just a guy who never knew the love of a family. I imagine what my life would have been like if Amanda hadn't taken me away from the orphanage in Lost Souls. A sector group would have taken me for sure, and then who would I have had? My only validation would have come from the sector's leaders and personnel, who would have wanted nothing more than to use me for their benefit. Stratton was younger than me when the Vernon Society took him into their ranks. He had no choice but to do what they said in order to survive, and then Laney and Talik pretended to accept and take care of him. For the first time, Stratton thought he'd felt love, and tried to keep it the only way he knew how.

Inside, he's just a desperate, lost child.

He's what I might have become if Amanda hadn't been there for me.

The thoughts form a blanket of dark clouds inside me as we walk in silence through the towering buildings of Seattle. Caiden doesn't say a thing, and neither does anyone else. Guns remain out as everyone stays on high alert.

"We're a mile away from the headquarters," Leeyah says at last, keeping her voice down.

I send my awareness out into the surrounding area after Envee glances at me with a silent signal to do so. Amplified by her, my consciousness sweeps through the brick structures ahead.

And I detect *hundreds* of people. These, unlike the Harvesters, are awake and focused on more than just the next meal. There's a lot of tension in the air and on every floor of the apartment complexes. Most people are inside, but others gather on the streets below in groups. These people know there's an attack coming, and some of them might have heard the distant FlexVipers going down. My reach doesn't quite touch the headquarters, but I've sensed enough.

"There really are hundreds of Society members," I say, opening my eyes. "How many of them are implanted?"

Leeyah faces me, but speaks to everyone. "I don't know about the ordinary citizens, but I'm sure all of the guards and fighters they have are implanted. Otherwise, their captured Influencers would have escaped by now."

Standing on my tiptoes, I try to see ahead. The fog's burning away in the morning sun, but before I can make out anything in the wide, cracked street, Leeyah waves everyone to the sides. We shuffle off the street and flatten around pillars and alcoves. Farren grasps my hand and peeks out around the structure.

"A blockade," he tells me. "The Society has one set up ahead."

Leeyah and Amanda stand opposite me. My curiosity burns, and I look around Farren. Far up the street, about half a mile, stands a wall of rusty, parked cars. The fog continues to thin, giving us a better view of the blockade. Flashes of red reveal Society beanies behind the wall of metal—at least a dozen of them. The fog and Leeyah's fast thinking may be the only reason they haven't spotted us yet.

"We need higher ground to stake out the area," Caiden says. "We can't see the side streets from here."

Ava nods. "I don't sense anyone in these buildings." She waves a tattooed arm at the ones sheltering us. "They must have been Harvester territory."

Leeyah agrees it's a good idea, and orders the two sides to climb to the top and look at the area. "Do not venture to the rooftops or balconies," she warns. "We do not want them to see us coming."

I follow Farren into the new apartment building. Caiden and Jax come along after us. The front door has long since been unlocked, and only has a fraying rope hanging from the door handle. Farren grips it and turns it over in his hand. It looks as if it's been used from inside to latch the door to a metal hook on the wall, a primitive lock. The Harvesters using it have left, not bothering to secure the door.

On the other side of the street, Amanda, Leeyah, Ava and the others vanish into a dark doorway. No one dares turn on a flashlight.

No gunfire erupts as I climb with Farren and Caiden up several floors. Unlike the ravaged building we took shelter in before, this one has paintings on the walls. Someone here took the time to make it feel like home.

Perhaps not all of the Harvesters are dulled down and just care about survival.

"You'll see what I was talking about," Stratton says, trailing up the stairs behind us. I hadn't realized he was following us. Caiden's starting to trust him enough to not keep a gun aimed at him at all times, but a scowl comes over his face as Stratton speaks.

At last, we reach the fifteenth floor. On sore legs, I follow Caiden into an apartment facing the direction of the blockade. This one has curtains over the sliding door. Caiden parts them a little and peers outside. I wait with the others and several of the Protectors as he makes his assessment.

"It's not good," he says at length. "That blockade isn't the only one. From here I see at least five others. The Society has set them up at every street we could possibly use to reach the headquarters."

"Let me see," I say.

Caiden warns me not to part the curtains too far, but it's enough to peek through them with one eye. Since we're high off the ground, it's easy to spot the blockades he's talking about. I count the five he mentioned, then spot a sixth through the thinning fog. The outline of the headquarters towers above everything else like the castle of a malevolent emperor. There are also groups of black and red specks on the rooftops of other apartment buildings. The Society has scattered its guards through the area surrounding the headquarters, and likely rallied some of its citizens to help. On this side of the headquarters alone, there must be a hundred of them, and they're all immune to Influencers.

I close the curtains, trying not to let the welling balloon of despair overtake me, but it's hard. Even Talas wasn't guarded this well. "What do we do now?"

Jax scratches his chin. "We'll need another approach."

"I wasn't lying to you about their forces," Stratton says with an air of satisfaction.

Farren paces in the living room. I watch as he peeks outside, studies the horror, and closes the curtains again. "We might have an advantage," he says. "Caiden, hear me out, please. The new toy, remember?"

"Yes!" he says, as if just remembering.

Farren removes his backpack. "Owen has a new invention that he gave to us before we left for Seattle."

Our tech guy is the one who came up with the block disruptors that helped save Caiden's life when we rescued Amanda, and makes those who have block implants vulnerable to Influencers for a period of time. If he has something new, I want to know about it, otherwise *none* of us will be proceeding to the Vernon Society.

Setting down his backpack, Farren pulls out something that looks like a large gun with a wide barrel. I've never seen anything like it before. He pulls out something shaped like a black grenade next and stuffs it into the barrel. Stratton takes a couple steps closer, eyeing the weapon with curiosity.

"What is this?" I ask. "A grenade launcher?"

Farren doesn't smile. "This is a block disruptor EMP bomb," he says to me and Jax. "When fired, it should have a much larger radius of effect than the block disruptors. Owen says it has the capability to disable all block implants for a full mile around the detonation. That will leave the Society's fighters vulnerable to Influencers."

"Why didn't we use that at the apartment?" I ask.

Caiden grins. "We had to save this for when there were no other options. I almost used it on the FlexViper pilots, but I'm glad I never got the chance."

Farren nods. "If I had fired it inside that apartment, there's a chance I wouldn't't've been able to aim it out the window. With us pinned behind that couch together, the explosion could have killed us all. And Owen was only able to give me one bomb—the prototype. We needed to save it for an occasion like this."

"Farren," I breathe.

Owen had given him the most valuable known weapon in the world.

Or Farren had taken it from him by force.

He holds me in a serious gaze. "However," he says, "there *is* a problem with using this." He takes his thumb and points to his chest. "This bomb will disable *all* block implants in the area."

Silence hangs. I swallow hard.

"Including yours," I say.

"Yes," Farren confirms. "I will be just as vulnerable as everyone else."

My heart races with the thought of that. Until now, no Influencer has been able to threaten Farren directly. It will be different once he fires that gun over the headquarters.

If Farren fires that gun, this fight will be up to the Influencers.

"We need to talk to Leeyah," I say. "She needs to know about this before we do anything. Ava and Envee, too."

We climb back down the stairs, Farren with the bomb launcher in hand. Leeyah and Amanda are already on the ground floor with Nance, and we have to speak across the road to each other to avoid being seen by the distant guards at the first blockade. Keeping his voice down, Farren tells Leeyah the deal, and her face hardens as she soaks up the information. He has to repeat himself three times.

"What do you think, Jax?" she asks. "Kaylin?"

Amanda shifts, uncomfortable, but she stays quiet. Farren wraps his arm around my waist and pulls me to his strong body. His touch tells me he's going to support me no matter my opinion on the matter.

"There's no other way forward but to use the EMP," I say.

Jax nods. "I agree. Ava? Envee?"

Ava looks at me before speaking. "I agree with Kaylin. We have a mission to protect and improve this world, and we need to do it however we can. If we can Push those guards, we'll have a chance to reach Laney and Talik."

"I'm ready to go," Envee says, bouncing in place.

Leeyah lets out a breath. "Then this will be a battle between Influencers. Whoever has the strongest, wins."

21

EYES WIDE

WITHOUT A WORD, Farren steps away from the pillar of the apartment building.

"Watch out," I whisper, even though the blockade is a half mile down the street.

Farren raises the launcher toward the sky as if he's aiming at the Vernon Society headquarters. Tremors overtake his arm. I can tell he knows what sort of danger he's in once he fires this weapon.

The others remain silent and I tense, waiting for the detonation. Farren grips the weapon with both hands, counts to three, and fires.

A loud *boom* makes me jump as his weapon recoils in his hands and nearly strikes him in the face. Smoke rises from the barrel. Once Farren regains his composure, I follow his gaze to the sky.

A faint smoke trail arcs above the city, sailing higher and higher until it seems that it'll reach the heavens. The fog has lifted and parted enough to reveal some blue sky, and as if trying to escape, the bomb soars through an opening.

And detonates with a loud eruption.

A bright flash bursts into sprawling electrical discharge, forcing me to look away until it dims. Gasps rise from the Protectors, but I focus on Farren. He grasps his head and jerks as if someone's struck him, squeezing his eyes shut. Caiden holds a hand over his eyes, watching the development. The Protectors squint, but appear unaffected by the EMP bomb. Only those with block implants have felt the shock.

The light leaves an afterimage floating in my vision. It's then that I realize I can now *feel* Farren's presence. Where there was silence before, there's a new type of warmth, different from the one that Leeyah gives off when she's near me. Farren's warmth is ecstasy.

"It's done," Farren announces. He looks right at me, features hard. He's trying to communicate the seriousness of this with his gaze. I have the job of protecting him as we march closer to the Vernon Society—and the job of protecting everyone. Until now, I hadn't realized that a few of the Protectors also had block implants, but I can feel them now, their consciousnesses joining with everything else as they await orders.

"Then we proceed, beginning with the blockade in front of us," Jax says. "Envee, with you amplifying us, we might be able to get them to drop their guns and surrender from here. The rest of you, don't harm the guards unless absolutely necessary. Kaylin, if you can recruit a few flocks of birds, you may be able to deal with those guards on the rooftops."

I nod, but the new flood of consciousness is trying to distract me. The world ahead feels more alive, fuller than it did before. Many of the Society's citizens don't have block implants to begin with, leaving them open for detection, but with the guards' implants disabled, I now feel twice as many living beings scattered up ahead. It's as if I've opened the door to a party after only hearing the muffled sounds from another room.

Strings of invisible tension pull at me. The guards know that something's wrong. If they're like Farren, they felt their block implants getting disabled.

"I can sense them now," Ava says. "The guards. They're open. We're more aware."

Stratton steps into the street, his dark eyes trained on the blockade ahead. "The Society's Influencers are just as aware as us. They know what we've done."

"Then we need to move," Jax says. "Kaylin, you need to guard the Protectors as well. I'll calm the blockade ahead. Ava, drive the others to flee and clear the way. Leo, try not to kill. Make them give up instead if you can. The rest of you, move forward. Together. Don't shoot unless you have to."

Stratton's expression darkens. "I'll try."

Will he be able to do that?

In two lines, we hug both sides of the street, staying in the cover of the buildings as much as we can. Envee walks beside Ava, amplifying her, and I see the red beanies of the guards ahead scrambling around in terror. Stratton remains silent, closing his eyes in concentration every few seconds. I know that, likely out of sight, he's sensing the weakest people in the buildings and making them surrender. That's *if* he's toning things down.

It's more difficult to Influence with my eyes open, but Envee's power washes over me, and I find that I can focus with more clarity than I ever have. On the other side of my eyelids, my consciousness expands over the city ahead, wrapping around the buildings like an advance of high water. My liquid awareness invades the windows of the surrounding apartment buildings, detecting the presence of Society citizens peeking down at us through the windows.

I feel concentration. A sense of hiding. Images flash behind my eyelids with every blink. I'm high above the street, looking down at the advancing Protectors as they attempt to hide in the shadows of the city. With gloved hands, he points a rifle at Leeyah—

A sniper.

Grasping him in ethereal fingers, I tell him that he needs to flee the room. He needs to drop his gun and leave the area. It's possible that Stratton will do worse to him, and I don't want that. Fear fills the man's chest and he turns away from the window, tossing his weapon behind an ancient, moldy couch and bolting for the stairs.

Breathing a sigh of relief, I retract my awareness and focus on the nearby buildings.

"I sense a group of snipers on a rooftop three buildings away and to our left," Jax says, interrupting me.

"Take cover!" Caiden shouts.

We press against buildings, ducking deep into the mid-morning shadows. My Push retracts, leaving me stuck in physical reality as my heart races. A shot fires in the distance, sparks shooting off the pavement only feet from where I stand. Amanda gasps and seizes my arm. She carries a weapon, but lacks the determination of the other well-trained fighters in our group.

I search for Farren and find that he's on the other side of the street, eyeing the blockade. He's left me with Jax. We've halved the distance to the blockade, and the guards behind the toppled cars have fled thanks to Ava.

"Kaylin, focus," Jax says behind me. "Send birds."

I close my eyes and take a breath, forcing my heart to calm. While I've grown better at sending out my Pushes, fear cuts into my concentration, but I manage to expand my awareness into the sky.

Only emptiness greets me. The sky is an expanse of nothing.

"The bomb scared away the birds," I say. "We'll need other animals."

"I've got this!" Stratton shouts, gripping a pillar on the other side of the street. "You won't like it, but we're going to do this."

Keeping my eyes closed, I forget about the animals and think of what Stratton has planned instead. I feel my consciousness expand even further with Envee's help, and I detect the tense, focused consciousness of four snipers at the top of a nearby building. They're waiting for us to emerge with bated breath, and I sense worry and dread coming from them.

Then a new sensation enfolds us all—a too-familiar dread and thick despair. The sensation coming from the snipers turns to a painful, murky black. Stratton's using his Push in the only way he knows how.

"No," I say. My voice sounds like it's in another universe as I remain focused on the rooftop, trying to enfold the snipers in a protective cocoon and turn their thoughts to surrendering their weapons. But, like me, Stratton's Push has been amplified to a terrifying degree. Thoughts of hopelessness and ending it all emanate from the snipers.

"They're jumping!" Nance shouts.

His words force my eyes open. On the other side of the street, the others watch the horror unfold. Envee's eyes fly open and her pupils dilate as she realizes what she's helped do. Four horrific smacking sounds, one after the other, follow from the direction we need to go.

Bodies hitting the ground. I hadn't thought they'd sound that way.

The snipers have thrown themselves off the building.

Stratton opens his eyes. He faces Leeyah, who stares at him with sadness and dismay. But this time, his expression is different. A shred of regret now inhabits his dark eyes as he lets out a breath.

"I could have handled that," I say, eyeing Envee.

Envee hyperventilates. "He made them kill themselves." She backs against the brick wall and sucks in a shaky breath. Envee's helped with plenty of Pushes before in battle, but this is the first time she's connected with Stratton.

No one says anything at first, but Jax nods in the direction of the street. "I don't detect any more snipers. They've fled from the tops of all the buildings after witnessing Leo's Push. We're close to the headquarters. We need to focus all our attention there. It seems that most of the guards have retreated to the tower."

Stratton rocks back on his heels with an air of satisfaction. Vile or not, making those snipers throw themselves to the pavement has had an effect.

It's an ugly reminder of the dark side of Influencers.

"Are you sure it's safe?" Farren asks. "Most of us are no longer protected by block implants."

"Keep fatalities minimal!" Leeyah shouts to everyone. "Allow Caiden, Nance, and Farren to march in the lead. I will follow. Influencers, stay at the back of the group and follow Jax's orders. Move. Now!"

She waves me behind the Protectors. Amanda gives me a shove in that direction, which I obey. Leeyah has a point. There's no reason for us to march in the front where Laney and Talik would see us before the others.

Envee and Ava join me. My heart aches at the thought of leaving Farren on the front lines, where he's most vulnerable. He peers over the other Protectors and gives me a reassuring nod, but it does little to dispel the worry and tension in my gut.

"Envee, are you okay?" Ava asks.

"I'm fine," she replies, collecting herself. "I'm tougher than I look."

Ava gives Stratton a sideways glare. "Try not to kill too many people."

Stratton swallows. "Understood."

"All right," Jax says as the Protectors form three lines in front of us. "Everyone's block implants are still down. Farren isn't sure how long the effect will last. Our next target is the headquarters. The guards who haven't fled have holed up there." He turns to Stratton. "I'm feeling out the building and Leo's right that there are ten Influencers inside on the top floor. I sense Laney and Talik up there as well. They outnumber us, but we have a good, talented team."

I wonder if Jax gets a feeling of warmth from the two of them, or if he just feels something dark in its place.

"Birds are out," I say, partly to distract him from the anguish of what he needs to do. "I'll see if I can find other animals who will help us."

"Good," Jax says. "Leo, find the weak people inside the headquarters and make them give up, but don't make them kill themselves unless they're about to kill one of us. Envee, you know your job. Ava, fill that headquarters with unbearable nightmares. Make the Society see the horror of what it's done to others."

Ava's expression is hard as she gives Jax a nod. "I will."

Jax swallows. "Do not kill Laney and Talik. If you can, avoid using a Push on them."

I can almost see his thoughts going back to Leeyah's explanation of Laney's insane behavior. Using a Push on her might make her claw her way deeper into madness.

With a hand signal, Leeyah orders us to move. My legs carry me closer to the towering headquarters, which waits at a T-junction at the end of the street. Its windows reflect the sun, hiding the horrors within. So far, I don't feel anything from the Influencers inside. What are they waiting for?

"There are guards stationed on each floor," Jax says as I close my eyes. "They're at the stairwells. We can assume they've cut power to the elevators."

I send out my awareness once again, blanketing the ground rather than the sky. A scattered army of bright pinpricks burst to life, some below ground and others above. Rats, stray dogs, other small animals, all foraging and trying to survive. I implore them to help us. There's food inside the headquarters if only they can fight their way to the top. The guards inside are keeping it from them. It's the most basic need of all, one these creatures can understand, and all at once a surge of movement rushes out of subway tunnels, alleyways, and abandoned buildings. A raging river of light races for the entrance, joined by tributaries and streams of small feet.

Lowering my awareness, I merge with them, and the skyscraper towers overhead as I rush along pavement and meet closed glass doors. Rats and dogs and cats claw at the glass, piling up on each other, desperate to enter. In another world, Jax shouts another command, but squeaks, growls, and barks mince his words.

From inside, the window shatters. I pour into the lobby and past boarded-up walls. There's a guard in black pointing a gun at the glass with a blank look in his eyes. Someone's Push has allowed the animals inside. He stands still as creatures pour over his feet. A stairwell enters my vision and I turn the tide to the steps as more guards scatter out of the way, firing into the living flow, but it's too much for them. The men go down, screaming, as the rats and other creatures of the city race over them, rising into the tower.

A second team of Vernon guards wait at the second level, before a row of apartments, when I reach the top, but none of them open fire. One bursts into tears and throws his weapon on the floor, beating his fist against the carpet. Another aims at invisible phantoms on the ceiling, pupils dilated in terror. I sense the despair and terror coming from them, and I sense more guards above thanks to Envee's help. The pressure from the living river builds behind me. More animals are desperate to reach the top, but even while I'm focused on the flow, I can sense many more guards above us, and the powerful, very aware presence of the Influencers—supernovas in a galaxy of regular stars.

The animals need to hurry. There isn't much time. The legion of small paws race up the stairway to the third floor—

A mental impact slams into me, and for a moment, I feel as if I'm falling. Light flashes in my mind from the blow and I blink, back on the street. The sun beats into my eyes as the headquarters continues to tower overhead. We've drawn closer. Jax holds my arm, guiding me. He blinks. Envee looks at me, confused. Ava sucks in a breath and whirls as if trying to get her bearings. Stratton utters a curse. Ahead of us, the Protectors continue to march forward as we stand there, lagging behind.

Something has ended my Push. There's no longer any sense of the people ahead. The mental silence is deafening.

Stratton eyes our target and speaks with hatred. "Neira. She's interfering with us."

Jax's eyes widen as he realizes the truth. "We had to expect this," he starts. "Everyone, we need to try a collective Push to shut her down. Envee, amplify us."

"I can't sense anyone," she shouts, panic taking hold.

From ahead, Caiden cries, "Take cover!"

A deafening *boom* follows from the direction of the building. I whirl in time to see smoke rising from an open window of the tower. A high whine fills the air as a shell flies from the headquarters, seeking its target, and a torrent of gunfire begins.

22

RETHINK

RAGING GUNFIRE FORCES all of us back. Hand in hand with Farren, I run away from the Vernon Society headquarters and duck into the cover of a restaurant awning. It won't protect us. It will only hide us from the eyes of the non-Influencers in the Society building above.

"It was a trap!" Caiden shouts. "They let us draw close!"

He's right. Neira waited until we were within sight of the Society's shooters to use her Push to disable ours.

The gunfire continues. Everyone presses into alleys and under overhangs. Bullets rain and drive up sparks from the cracked pavement. Something explodes up the street where we stood seconds ago. The Society's firing mortars from somewhere, and with Neira blocking our

Pushes, I can't tell where it's coming from. She's blinded us.

"Everyone!" Leeyah shouts. She yanks a radio off her belt and speaks into it. "Do you copy? We need to spread out our Pushes and make it harder for Neira to stop us all. I doubt her reach can go very far. With Envee's help, we may be able to get an advantage again. Stopping this fire is priority."

I try to reach out and feel the city's animals again, but Neira's left me with the senses of a non-Influencer. I turn my attention to Farren, but his deep brown eyes remain clear.

"The FlexViper might be useful at this point," Caiden shouts. He stands behind Farren. "A few of us need to run back to it. Ava, Envee, follow me. We'll circle around to the east of the building. Someone needs to attack from the west and someone else from the front. Do you think Neira can stop Influencers from three angles?"

"I don't know," Leeyah says. "She would need an amplifier like Envee." She repeats Caiden's plans into her radio.

On the other side of the street, the others remain hidden in the alleyways and under other cover. Amanda's with them, holding her gun and pressing into a brick corner. Gunfire misses her by inches. Another mortar explodes, closer than the last, and the smoke from it drifts past as pieces of concrete rain down. Then the gunfire calms, as if the fighters have realized they have no chance of hitting us right now.

"I can take the west with some fighters," Jax says. He nods to Leeyah. "Is it possible to get there while remaining hidden?"

"Yes."

"Then me and Leo take the front?" I ask. The thought of charging the front of the Society headquarters is terrifying and makes my heart race. It will be slow and dangerous. Ava and Envee might be safer than the rest of us in the FlexViper.

"I'm going with you," Farren says, tightening his grip on my arm. He holds me in a loving but protective glare. He doesn't want me to go with Stratton alone, and I'm glad for that. No argument manages to escape my throat. The two of us are meant to fight together, and always have been.

"It's settled," Leeyah says, fixing me in with that same protective look, but there's no longer any time for family ties or affection. Separating is the only chance we have against the Vernon Society and Neira. My heart aches at the thought of us possibly not seeing each other again, but Ava's right. We Influencers play a key role in shaping our reality for the better. We have to split up.

Caiden, Ava, and Envee backtrack, sticking to the sides of buildings and heading back around the first blockade to where the FlexViper waits far down the street. The Vernon fighters in that direction have already fled and retreated to the main fortress, leaving them safe until they get in the air. With Caiden leading them, Ava and Envee are in good hands.

A single shot fires and bounces off the pavement nearby, but none follow. Leeyah waits a moment to be sure, then bolts across the street with Jax, staying low. Another bullet follows, but misses by feet. The Society knows we're hiding here, even without Caiden giving his tactical input. After another minute, Leeyah waves some of the Protectors, including Amanda, across the street to me and Farren and Stratton. Then she appears to think and waves several more over to me. Just like Farren, she wants to protect me, and is doing it in the only way she can right now.

The Protectors have to run across the street one at a time to avoid getting hit by gunfire. The tactic works, and Amanda joins me, holding her gun to her chest. "This is it," she breathes, casting a dark look at Stratton.

"You're going to hang back with the other non-Influencers," Farren says to her and everyone else once we have two dozen fighters lined up behind us. "I'll give you the signal to move to the tower when Kay and Leo think it's safe."

Amanda looks as if she wants to bite her lip, but she backs away and joins the line of young, black-clad fighters.

"So we just wait?" I ask.

Farren nods. "Yes. Caiden will radio me once they believe Neira is distracted enough to let you use your Push again."

A couple of large rats scurry past us, spooked by the gunfire. The animals are trying to flee from the action. My heart aches when I think of how many of them might have fallen to the Vernon Society. I'm using these innocent beings as sacrifices. They didn't choose to join this war.

No one speaks as we wait. Leeyah and Jax wave their own team of fighters into the alley and vanish into the alleyway, heading towards the western part of the Society's territory.

"We need to be able to see," I say. "We can't tell what's happening at the HQ."

"She's right," Stratton agrees. "Waiting here, being blind, is not working."

Farren glares at him for a long moment before nodding. "We can enter another building, so long as we maintain cover. It's better than staying on this street. All of you, follow me."

The restaurant we enter isn't tall enough to afford us much of a view, and only offers rooftop dining, according to the faded sign in the window, so we have to backtrack further to a taller former office building. I try to sense any people left inside, but my ability's still neutered by Neira. As we climb the steps, I watch Farren and Amanda for any signs of a Push from one of the Society's Influencers, but I detect nothing out of the ordinary. Perhaps they don't have someone who can amplify them, or we're just out of reach.

Or perhaps they're waiting to spring another trap if we make it into the building. That seems to be what the Society is fond of—surprises.

At last, we make it to the ninth and top floor of the office building. This must be one of the structures Ava and Stratton cleared out, because there are sniper rifles lying on the floor. The team picks them up. Farren waves us towards an office window with closed blinds. We crowd before it, and I part one of the blinds and peek through.

Now that the fog has lifted, I have a perfect view of the Vernon Society headquarters, realizing how close we are. The headquarters is only a few buildings away. I can see the mortars, which look like small cannons, posted on top of the roof. There's also something that looks like a raised Viper pad up there. Several Society members in red and black gather around it as if waiting for Laney and Talik to make an escape.

"Where's the FlexViper?" I ask.

"It's coming," Farren assures me. "I hope those things have bad aim."

"I'm still blocked," Stratton mutters with disgust. "Neira won't ever come to our side. If I find her—"

I spot something black in the air, emerging from the low clouds. Caiden's piloting the FlexViper. At first, nothing happens as he circles. No one fires on the new arrival.

"They must think the Viper's giving them backup," Farren says. "Caiden's making them think they're on the Society's side. That will give Ava and Envee time to work. Kay, Leo, try to use your abilities again."

I close my eyes, knowing that beside me, Stratton is doing the same. My consciousness is still trapped inside my own head. With each breath, I attempt to use my Push, but Neira's blanket remains over us. She must know that we're in this area, and is focusing on me and Stratton, but she might not know that—

"They're scattering!" Farren says. "Ava and Envee are coming through!"

His voice compels me to open my eyes. They adjust to the sunlight and I spot the Society fighters running off the Viper pad as if in terror. More fighters abandon the mortars. They point their guns at an invisible monster in the air and fire, wasting their ammunition on the clouds. The FlexViper continues to make large, looping circles over the eastern side of the building.

"It won't be long before Neira realizes she needs to redirect her attention," Farren says.

"You feel anything?" Amanda asks me.

"I don't—"

But then there's a sense as if Neira's blanket has lifted and the world is clear again. Farren's protective warmth flows over me. My awareness has returned. Stratton lifts one eyebrow at me, and I know the same has just happened for him.

Farren's radio crackles before I can close my eyes. Caiden's voice comes through.

"Ava and Envee are at work. The mortars are disabled. We're focusing on ending the fire. Move forward!"

"She's overwhelmed," Farren says. "Leo, Kaylin, now's the time to reach the entrance of the Society. They're distracted, and we might not get another chance."

Our team bolts down the steps, which makes it impossible for me to send out a concentrated Push, but Stratton remains silent, and I'm sure he's attempting one. It's not until we reach the bottom of the stairs that I'm able to increase my focus and shift it into the inside of the headquarters. I sense that it's empty save for some scattered rats and dogs. The personnel of the building have retreated to the top floors to launch their surprise attack.

Farren orders us to keep to the sides of the building in case some of the fighters or the Influencers themselves are still able to shoot at us from the upper windows. I've forgotten how tall the Vernon Society building is. The hum of the FlexViper intensifies as the black shape hovers over us, casting papers and other debris out of the way, and then lands on the top of the building. Caiden and the others are trying to keep Laney and Talik from escaping by air.

My awareness remains as we press closer to the shattered front doors. A few more rats and dogs burst out and flee past us. I let them go. We might need them later, but I don't want to alert the Society that we're drawing close to the front doors. Not yet. Caiden would say that wasn't a good idea.

The gunfire remains absent. I feel Neira's blanket try to sweep over me again, cutting off my consciousness from the rest of the world, but it only lasts for a couple of seconds before clearing. The other Influencers have her distracted and unable to deal with us all at once now that we're in different places. Caiden says something over the radio about stopping the gunfire as Farren waves us across the street. In two lines, our team bolts over the pavement and through the shattered doors. More rats scatter and hide in the shadows of the lobby.

"We're inside," Farren says into the radio.

"Won't they be able to pick up our communications?" Amanda asks.

"Yes," Farren says, whirling to check out the whole room. Potted plants are knocked over, spilling leaves and dirt over the floor. "But we have no other way."

Neira's Push cuts me off again, but Stratton shoves me back into Farren, then faces the lobby's front desk. A pair of Society fighters rise from behind it and aim at Stratton. He jumps between me and the ambush, spreading his arms. One of the men fires, and Stratton's arm jolts as a bullet makes impact. Blood rises like lava from an angry volcano, but he remains still and focuses on the two fighters, who now stare at him, jaws falling open. He's using his Push. Neira might be focused on me, but somehow she doesn't realize that he's here. Her attention is too scattered.

"It's Stratton," the first fighter says in terror.

The second fighter throws down his gun, and one of the Protectors confiscates it. "They're going to win," the fighter says in despair. "We might as well surrender."

My awareness returns, and I realize that several more fighters are charging down from the second floor. I sense them before I hear their footfalls on the steps. The first fighter behind the counter also throws down his weapon and Stratton whirls, blood dripping down his arm, to face the steps. Guns cock around me as everyone faces the new wave of Society fighters. Another terrified rat races over my foot.

"Don't shoot!" I shout at the Protectors, thinking of how Farren reacts to things.

Farren pushes me back as several Society members stand in the gloom, taking aim, but Stratton remains in front of us, focusing his Push, and all but two fighters freeze, lowering their guns. Closing my eyes, I send out my awareness. I detect the tense consciousness of the Protectors, a tight web of fear and determination. Pushing out beyond it, I wrap around the Vernon fighters, sensing growing despair and fear. Stratton's dread pumps through their web like poison, threatening to spill over to the Protectors. I focus on the two remaining fighters, a man and a woman who are better able to resist Stratton's spell, and focus thoughts of surrender and peace into their minds. They resist me at first, then I sense their resistance melting as they lay down their arms. Flashes of the lobby enter my vision as I merge with them.

"We surrender!" one of the men shouts, his voice barely above tears.

"They're Pushing us!" the strong woman yells.

Focusing harder, I enfold the woman as Stratton continues to work. But it's no use. Someone fires, yanking me out of the Push, and my vision adjusts in time to see the woman go down, blood spurting from her leg.

"No!" I gasp, looking to Farren. He holds his gun at her, smoke rising from the barrel.

"She was going to shoot you," he says. "But I think she'll live."

The rest of the Vernon fighters lay down their arms, and one man collapses and curls into a fetal position, silent tears flowing over his cheeks. Amanda seizes weapons and passes them out to our fighters, who take them in silence. Stratton lowers his arms. Blood continues to soak through his left sleeve. He looks down at it and shock comes over his features. Until now, he hadn't realized his injury.

"You're hurt," I say over the sobs and groans of the disabled fighters.

"But none of you are."

"You saved my life," I tell him.

Farren lowers his gun and faces Stratton, biting his lip like he wants to say something, but this time he doesn't.

"Does anyone have any first aid supplies?" I ask, whirling. The other Protectors are busy aiming at the Society members in case they have hidden weapons and searching pockets. Amanda and two others guard the staircase, ensuring that no one else comes down after us. Others work on binding the wrists of the Vernon Society fighters with old handcuffs and zip ties. Leeyah has ensured that we are able to take prisoners rather than kill them.

But Stratton's already working, tearing his opposite shirt sleeve apart. Without complaint, he rips off a strip and hands it to me, waiting in silence. This is a man used to no one caring about him, someone who knows better than to complain. He waits for someone to do what they need to do to keep him functioning.

I tie the strip around his arm, keeping my consciousness expanded to the next couple of floors and the basement below. No one else tries to charge down at us. Either Ava, Jax, and Envee are keeping them distracted, or they have another trap ready.

"I think that'll stop the bleeding," Stratton says, nodding a silent thanks. "I'll keep these fighters incapacitated for as long as I can."

"Thanks," Farren says with great effort. His radio crackles again.

"*We've stopped all enemy fire*," Caiden says. "*Jax and Leeyah's team is now advancing on the tower. What is your position?*"

"Front lobby," Farren says into it. "Code Orange."

"What does that mean?" I ask once he lowers the radio.

"We're going to charge up," Farren says to all of us. "It's time to find Laney and end this."

23

RETRIBUTION

PROGRESSING UP THE Vernon Society tower is exhausting and terrifying. As we move from floor to floor, my legs threaten to give out from exhaustion. The power to the elevators has been cut, but it's no real surprise. Once we reach the fifth floor, Leeyah tries to call one to see if the Vernon fighters could use it, but the lights above the doors don't work, and no hum follows when she presses the buttons.

"They don't want us to use the elevators," she says. "That means the Society can't use them, either. But they have the advantage of attacking us from above. Stay sharp, everyone."

At least Leeyah and Jax's team have joined us before making the final ascent. Neira's Push comes and goes, cutting off my awareness from everyone else. That's a sign Ava and Envee are still on the roof, drawing her attention and Pushing the guards on the upper floors.

"Incoming!" Farren shouts, raising his weapon on the stairwell to the sixth floor. More Society guards pour down and the Protectors open fire. They have no choice but to take down these guards by force. I watch the five men crumple and jolt from the impact of the bullets. The sight sickens me, and I try to reach for my ability, but Neira's still holding me back. Doesn't she understand the more she does that, the more Society fighters have to die or be injured?

One of the Society fighters manages to get a shot off, striking one of the Protectors in the leg before he falls. The terrible noise dies and I stand there, my awareness returning. Tension from everyone else streams into my awareness and even Leeyah's warmth can't comfort me now.

Farren frowns at me. "I'm sorry."

"We had no choice," Leeyah says. "Ava and Envee are doing the best they can."

After progressing through the seventh and eighth floors, we find another group of Society guards awaiting us on the ninth. Neira's attention is not on us, so Stratton's able to make them give up in despair. I sense more guards on the tenth and eleventh floors, waiting to ambush us from the apartments, but I enfold them with an exhale and surround them with feelings of forgiveness. They resist, but lay down their arms with a sense of calm. There's no doubt that Jax is helping me.

"Bind the survivors," Leeyah orders, sadness in her voice. "We will take them with us when we leave. How's Caiden?"

"He's holding his own." Farren holds up the radio. "They're distracting the guards on the upper floors. We should have an easier time once we get there. Kay, we still need you to sense what's going on."

After progressing to the next floors and detaining the calm fighters we find waiting for us, hands held up in surrender, an ominous silence falls. We're close to the top floor. All of us study each other, mouths open, waiting. Neira's stopped trying to cut off our Pushes.

"What do you think Neira will try?" Leeyah asks Stratton.

"She's unpredictable," he says, keeping his voice low. Behind him, silent tears pour down a guard's cheeks as Stratton continues to subdue him with a Push. "Even I can't tell. We were only in each other's wonderful company for a few months."

"Then we need to stay sharp," Leeyah says to everyone. "Farren, is your block implant still down?"

He nods somberly. "She could try anything."

Neira's ability to create temporary Influencers comes back to my mind. When she wants, she can launch an attack on our entire team. Only I, Jax, Leeyah, and Stratton will be immune. I look at the Protectors assembled in the hallway, standing wherever the tied guards aren't taking up space. Leeyah opens her mouth like she's going to say something, but she pauses, then closes it again. Jax shifts foot to foot.

"We might need to use force," Leeyah says at last.

It's decided, then.

"Not on my parents," Jax pleads, pain at the very thought evident on his face. The Vernon fighters trying to fire on us has gutted him emotionally. Perhaps his parents don't realize he's here. They're not Influencers, after all.

"Not on your parents," Leeyah agrees. "I don't want harm to come to Laney. She needs help. My help. Come, we need to finish this."

No guards confront us while we traverse the next couple of floors. As we climb floor after floor, the sounds of terrified guards float through the closed doors. Ava's Push, though interrupted at times, is enough to clear the way for us. She's in the FlexViper with Caiden. Farren tells Caiden, over the radio, that we're almost to the top floor.

"Where are the other Influencers?" Farren asks.

There's no answer at first, but then Ava speaks over the radio. *"I made sure the guards mistook them for monsters. The guards fought back. Those Influencers weren't talented enough to react in time. They won't be in the way."*

A heavy silence falls over the stairwell. The closed door Farren puts his hand on tells us we're on the second to last floor while an arrow on the wall directs us to the top floor. Laney and Talik are waiting there.

"We only have Neira then," Leeyah says. "That means she's on the top floor. Laney and Talik must want her by their side. There must be few, if any guards left."

"Even Influencers are expendable to them," Stratton says.

Leeyah smiles at him. "You're not with them anymore."

Upon reaching the top floor, Farren shoots out the lock that holds the door shut. He looks at me gravely, telling me with his eyes to feel out the space beyond. I think of the marble floors and the luxurious gold trim of the headquarters, and with that thought my consciousness expands. Farren and Leeyah already pour through. I have to follow them and make sure they don't fall into a trap.

"No," Amanda says, brushing my arm with her hand.

I detect Neira's wall as my awareness cuts off, leaving me isolated. I freeze as the Protectors scramble through the door, following Farren and Leeyah. Catching my breath, I realize they're headed into danger.

I emerge in the marble chamber to find a ring of our fighters surrounding Leeyah. Slowly, as if in a trance, they point their weapons at her. Leeyah whirls, terror dilating her pupils. On the other side of the room stands Neira and Miya, guarding a door that leads to the rest of the top floor. Neira focuses her attention on the fighters, ready to single-handedly execute Leeyah.

"She's Pushing all of you!" I shout.

Farren grasps his head with his free hand before joining the ring and raising his gun at Leeyah. A look of pure agony sweeps over his face and his eyes tighten, shaking. I grasp his arm and scream his name.

"That's my mother!" I shout. "Don't kill her! Please Farren!"

Farren blinks as he rejoins the world. My voice has pulled him out of the Push.

And in a lightning fast motion, he points his gun at Neira.

She has no time to react other than to allow her mouth to fall open before he fires. Bullets scream through the room as sparks fly from the barrel of his weapon. Neira jolts as her blood splatters against the wall behind her. Her body tries to fall, but Farren maintains fire as Miya jumps back behind a pillar, taking cover. The Influencer's tattered form jumps over and over, and I find myself screaming at Farren to stop. Amanda seizes my arm and pulls me back.

At last, the gunfire dies. Farren lowers his weapon and looks and me, and then Leeyah, eyes wide with horror. He only wanted to protect me. Around us, the other Protectors lower their weapons as well. Silence falls as Neira bleeds out on the floor, an expanding red puddle dyeing the marble with the stain of war.

"Kay," Farren says softly, "I wasn't going to let her kill your mother."

"You snapped him out of it," Amanda adds.

Farren lets out a breath. Then all emotion leaves his face as he pulls out his radio and presses the button. "Neira is neutralized. Hold for orders."

"*Since when did* you *become the boss, Ferret?*" Caiden asks, amping up the agitation in his tone.

Caiden's jab does little to dissolve the tension in the room, but the air has also cleared of Neira's influence, allowing me to sense everything—the fear and sadness that fills the space. Leeyah steps away from the other Protectors as if fearing that Neira can perform another Push from beyond the grave. She stands next to Jax.

Miya emerges from behind the pillar, hands raised in surrender. The tiny, dark-haired woman trembles as her boots tap the marble floor. She faces Farren, eyes reddened with regret.

"Don't shoot," she pleads, stepping away from Neira's body.

Farren starts to lift his weapon again as he stands in front of me. "You brought Kay and Jax here," he says, voice low and dangerous.

"I know that I did. I betrayed you and the Resistance, and it was wrong. Hurting you was the last thing I wanted to do, Farren. It was never my intention." She takes a step closer to us.

"Secure her," Leeyah says.

I wait for Farren to shoot, but his expression softens. He waves to the other Protectors with his free hand, who move forward, guns raised. Miya turns and allows them to bind her with zip ties, her eyes downturned in guilt.

Leeyah shakes her head, regaining her composure. "I want a small team to confront Laney and Talik. Kaylin, do you sense any other guards on this floor?"

Now that Neira isn't cutting me off every few seconds, I'm able to close my eyes and focus. Though I'm shaking, that vanishes as I send out my Push to the rest of the floor. I sense our group, Miya, and three others deeper within the confines of the top floor. Laney and Talik are here with one other person.

"There are three people," I relay.

"Laney feels off to me," Jax adds.

"Then I think we should confront them without dozens of fighters," Leeyah says. The warmth coming from her ripples with tension. She wants to confront Laney on her own, without the help of everyone. It's a personal matter.

"I want Farren to come with us," I say. "And Amanda."

Amanda nods to me in approval. It only feels right if we do this together.

"Then we have an arrangement," Leeyah says. She turns to the other Protectors. "Go through the building and move our prisoners to the first blockade we encountered. We'll figure out what to do with them later. If you see any food supplies, take those, too, along with any non-combat staff that you find. Do *not* harm anyone unless necessary."

Nance gathers the other fighters, who head back down the steps. I'm left with Leeyah, Jax, Farren, Stratton, and Amanda. I'm surprised Stratton has remained, but I imagine he wants to confront Laney and Talik as well.

Without a word, we progress to the closed door. Farren remains silent now that Miya's gone. He shoots off the lock and kicks it open.

This is a different entrance than Jax and I used before, but the lavish decor around us tells me we're in the right place. This hallway has several hardwood doors and several tall fish tanks. I sense three people in a room to the left. Farren kicks that door open as well and we find a large living room complete with leather furniture, a radio, and several computer monitors on polished wood desks. A picture window looks out on the city below.

Laney, Talik, and Captain Relic stand in the middle of the room, unarmed. It's clear they expected us. I stand to the side, searching the apartment for cameras, but they must be hidden. It's not that different from the space Jax and I spent time in together when first arriving. Even now, a dish of chocolates stands on the glass end table, uneaten.

Laney has bags under her eyes. Talik stands near her, holding her hand, but otherwise trying to shrink back. Stratton's assessment of him appears to be true: Laney's the boss here. Even Captain Relic awaits her word.

Farren points his gun at him. "Don't move."

"Stratton?" Laney asks. "How could you betray me?"

Relic lifts one hand. His pistol waits on his hip.

Leeyah steps forward, silent at first, before lowering her weapon. Farren's covering for her. "Laney."

It's my cue to stand aside. This is for Leeyah and Jax.

Laney holds up a hand to Relic. "Stand down," she orders. "This is between me and Leeyah."

Relic glares at her as if she's crazy. "They will *destroy* the Society," he protests.

"I believe the Vernon Society is already destroyed," Laney replies. There's no hope in her voice. Instead, a scary calm has replaced the fight in her. She's different. What's happened between my escape and now?

Without a word, Amanda and Stratton walk over to Relic, who places his pistol on the end table, leaving it by the chocolates, as they bind him with another zip tie. Leeyah nods, and the two of them take him from the room. We listen as their footsteps fade. I imagine they're taking him to be with our other prisoners at the blockade.

They leave a thick silence in their wake. Now it's just me, Farren, Jax, and Leeyah. Jax takes a breath. He looks unsure of what to say. How would he even start?

"Laney," Leeyah says, "your hatred of Influencers hasn't stopped you from using them for your own purposes."

Laney glares at her sister. "You know why I've had to take the actions that I have."

"Laney, *think*," Leeyah pleads. "You have power here, and potential to do good. You could turn the Vernon Society into something that helps the world."

"If I didn't control them, someone else would!" she snaps, voice rising. Laney looks much younger for a moment, like a hurt child. "Look at what happened. You wouldn't listen to me. You wouldn't let me *help* you, and see what happened?"

"But what have you done?" Leeyah asks. "You've killed just as many as we have. Look at what you forced Leo Stratton to do."

"Think of what someone else would have made him do. The Magnus Order, when they still existed. The Southern Alliance. Those people would have used him against us."

"You could have protected him instead of using him," Leeyah counters.

Pressing against the wall, I realize there's nothing I can do except listen. Jax steps forward, standing in front of Leeyah. Laney looks at him and her gaze softens.

"Please, Mom," he says. "We're not walking weapons here to be picked up off the streets and stolen like objects. We're not guns and knives. We're *people*. I'm your son. I'm you." Jax eyes the door as if he wants to flee. My cousin is torn.

Talik looks to Laney, but his wife shakes her head.

"Jax—" Laney starts.

"Please forgive us." Talik's eyes moisten and redden. "Jax, Kay, we've done wrong here. Bringing you here by force and recruiting you against your will was a mistake."

Jax faces him. "I know you didn't want to do this. I hope to forgive you one day." He turns back to Laney. "Please. Think about what you're doing."

The redness in Talik's eyes softens. There's a dynamic here that I don't completely understand. Leeyah must have needed to protect herself in the past. But Laney shows no signs of opening up.

"Laney, listen to Jax," Leeyah urges. "He's making sense here."

"You don't understand what I've seen," Laney shouts, turning from Jax to Leeyah. Her eyes then skip to land on me. "Or what your mother did."

Leeyah takes a step back. This is more than mere jealousy, but I sense that asking Laney more about their past will not calm this situation. Even Jax can't get it under control. I think of using my Push, but that will only set Laney over the edge. She paces in front of her husband, working her lips like she wants to say something, so there's nothing we can do but wait. My heart races.

"Do you have something to say?" Leeyah asks with dread. "Say it."

"Yes, I tried to control the Influencers," Laney says at last. "But it did not work. Even Leo turned on us. People still died."

A device on Laney buzzes. She pulls out a handheld computer screen, paling as she reads whatever's on it. "The treaty," she says. "The other groups have detected our fall. Now they're fulfilling it."

"The treaty?" Jax echoes.

I remember Stratton mentioning the Vernon Society making deals with the other sector groups. This must be what he was talking about.

"We made an agreement with the other sector groups," Laney says, speaking quickly now. "In the event of the Society's fall, they would be allowed to remove our Influencers from the world to start the process of returning things to their previous state. In exchange, the other groups wouldn't attack us so long as we kept the Society together. But now we're over. Now the other groups will eliminate Influencers from existence."

"Remove Influencers?" Jax shouts.

Laney speaks as if trying to get out as much information as she can before something happens. "We had to protect ourselves. I didn't think you'd be here for it. I didn't think *I'd* see it. Two-thirds of all sector groups don't use Influencers. They fear them. And if I can't control them, then no one will."

"Mom," Jax starts, injecting immense pain into his voice, "you want to kill me?"

"You are family," Laney says, tears in her eyes. "You, Kay, and Leeyah. All of you. Get out. I'm staying. I've failed to control the Influencers. This is for the best."

"What do you mean?" I ask.

"The Southern Alliance is coming," Laney continues. "They've notified me of an airstrike to ensure that no Influencers survive. Go before they get here. Get as many blocks away as you can. Take your prisoners with you. There are many good souls in the Society who deserve to live. The Alliance won't know I'm staying."

Shock falls over the room. I feel as if someone's punched me in the stomach.

Leeyah reaches out to Laney. "Sis, can you stop it?"

"No," Laney says, avoiding her eyes. "It was part of the treaty. They've detected the destruction here, the deaths, the prisoners."

"Then escape with us!" Jax shouts. "Please, I found you again and I don't want to leave without you. You don't have to die!"

"There's no point. I can't fulfill my mission." Agony fills her eyes for a moment before settling into peace.

"Dad, come on," Jax says. "Talk to her."

Talik shakes his head. "She's right. My place is with your mother. Go. All of you!"

Leeyah takes my arm. "We have to leave. Jax, follow us. Farren, tell Caiden to take off and meet us when it's safe. Move!"

Leeyah pushes me to the apartment door and we burst into the hallway. Farren pulls a reluctant Jax from the room as he yells at Caiden to take Ava and Envee away from the headquarters. I glance back to see Laney and Talik standing by the glass table, hand in hand, watching us leave.

But there's no time to linger. With a pain in my chest, I run with the others to the stairwell, but see that the elevator's overhead light is working. It's been turned on for us. Laney and Talik are allowing us to escape as quickly as possible. I shout something now forgotten. We board and Farren radios to Nance to get everyone out of a several-block radius of the headquarters. Amanda responds that she's nearly to the blockade with Stratton, Miya, and Captain Relic. We're going to be the last escapees.

Farren seizes my hand as the elevator descends. Jax places his face in his hands, but no tears come. I want to hug him, and I will if we get out of this alive. Leeyah remains silent.

And then Jax growls in rage and strikes the wall of the elevator with his fist. I flinch, but no one reprimands him.

The doors open on the first floor. The Protectors have cleared out the prisoners. Even the animals have fled, as if sensing that death is coming from above. The four of us burst out from the broken Vernon Society headquarters and break into a full run down the street, heading toward the first blockade. It's hard to run—climbing the stairs sapped the strength from my legs—and Farren has to help steady me, but adrenaline propels me forward. Lungs burning, I bolt through block after block as my side tries to seize and make me collapse to the cracked pavement. A crowd waits behind the very first blockade. The black vests and red beanies of captured Society fighters wait. I glimpse Miya and Amanda near the front.

"Back!" Farren shouts, waving his free arm. "There's an airstrike!" His words are hoarse with effort.

The human mass shifts as panic takes over. A loud screech sounds from above, followed by another. A squadron of fast, large aircraft enters the airspace.

The Southern Alliance has arrived.

Farren yanks on my arm and pulls me behind the blockade of old cars as others scream and order each other to take cover.

The world explodes.

Farren pulls me close as we whirl and the Vernon Society headquarters disappears into fiery flowers and deafening *booms*. The apocalypse spreads, consuming the surrounding buildings and quaking the ground. Glass shatters around us from the shock waves, raining down, and Farren pushes me to the pavement and falls over me. Eternity stretches out as heat washes over us from the explosions. The world shakes. Protectors and Society members alike scream united in their terror.

But at last, the horrific noise dies.

I open my eyes and Farren says something about it being safe for me to stand. He sounds as if he's in another universe. He helps me up. A dark world of dust and smoke has replaced the old one. Coughing, I lean into Farren as he wipes grit from my cheeks.

"We made it," he says.

There's a small cut above his temple, but he's otherwise unscathed. This must be a dream. There's no way all these dust-covered beings walking around aimlessly are people. I glimpse a red beanie, part of a black vest, and Miya's tiny form standing nearby, but no bodies. All are silent as shock and numbness blanket everything. There's no need for my enhanced awareness to tell me that.

There's no longer a Society headquarters, or any of the surrounding structures, for that matter. The remaining pile of rubble smokes. Concrete, metal beams, and other materials belch fire into the sky, along with several other buildings in the surrounding blocks. The thought takes forever to form, but eventually it does.

The Southern Alliance has just taken out the Vernon Society headquarters. I had no idea they had this capability.

One last high-pitched whine follows an aircraft as it zooms past, and then there's nothing. The mission here is completed.

Laney and Talik didn't have to die. The Southern Alliance warned them. They could have escaped, but it wasn't part of the plan.

"Did everyone make it?" I blurt out, sure that I'll wake any time now.

"I think so," Farren says. "We need to see Jax."

Allowing him to lead me through the dust and broken glass that coats the street, I spot Jax leaning against a building, face buried in his hands. He's silent, overcome with emotion. Leeyah stands beside him, half-covered in dust. The redness in her eyes is obvious.

Numbness consumes me now. The emotion will hit later.

Leeyah waves us over. She swallows to hide her emotion and speaks. "Kay. Jax. The world has changed today, and not for the better. We have entered a new age of fear."

Farren pulls me to his side as if trying to protect me. Without him there, I'm sure I would break down.

"A new age?" I ask.

Leeyah nods. "The leaders of this region have made a decision, and that's to remove us from it. It will take everything we have to survive."

Despair and terror hits, making my heart race. Farren's the only thing holding me upright.

"What if they're right?" I ask. "What if the world would be a better place without us? It's *us* the corporations used to do this to the country." Tears flow and Farren lifts a gloved hand to wipe them away. Instead, he only smears the dust into mud.

"Kaylin, listen," Leeyah says. "Fear does things to people. It changes them. That's what happened to my sister when my family found out I was an Influencer. But maybe we evolved for a reason, as Ava likes to say. There could be a purpose for us that the rest of the world doesn't realize yet."

I nod, unable to speak. Jax remains facing the building, as if trying to hide from everyone. I sense that he wants us to leave him alone.

"You have the Protectors on your side," Leeyah continues. "We have fighters and talent and skill. We will do *everything* in our power to ease fear and bring peace back to this world. Come on, Kaylin. We need to move." She turns to the others. "We need to head out! Back to the research facility. And don't harm the prisoners. We've all had a tough day."

Farren kisses me, lips tickling my hair. "You don't scare me," he says. "I won't let fear turn me into a monster."

I still feel his expansive awareness. The implant's block has not yet returned. Maybe it never will.

"Thanks," I say, thinking of Laney and how she placed all the blame on Leeyah and the Influencers. It was non-Influencers who caused most of the conflicts, not the other way around.

Leeyah forces a smile onto her face. "Let's get moving. A new world awaits us, but as long as you're in my life, anything's possible."

She's right. What's to come is far more intimidating than anything I've faced before.

But now I have my real family by my side.

End of Book Two

***

Free Origin Novella and Updates on Book 3: Be the first to find out when book three of the Influence series will release. In addition, get 'Humanity's Protectors' (Influence Series Origin Novella) for free, giveaway opportunities, and other exclusive bonuses by joining my VIP List at www.davidrbernstein.com.

Thank you for reading book one of the Influence series. If you enjoyed reading this book, please remember to leave a review on Amazon. Positive reviews are the best way to thank an author for writing a book you loved. When a book has a lot of reviews, Amazon will show that book to more potential readers. The review does not have to be long—one or two sentences are just fine! I read all my reviews and appreciate each one of them!

www.davidrbernstein.com

Acknowledgements:
ial thanks to my wife for her support on this journey! I
love you.
Thanks to all my family for the support!

Credits:
Chase Night - Editor
Jack Llartin - Editor
Torment Publishing